The Girls of Lighthouse Lane

Lizabeth's Story

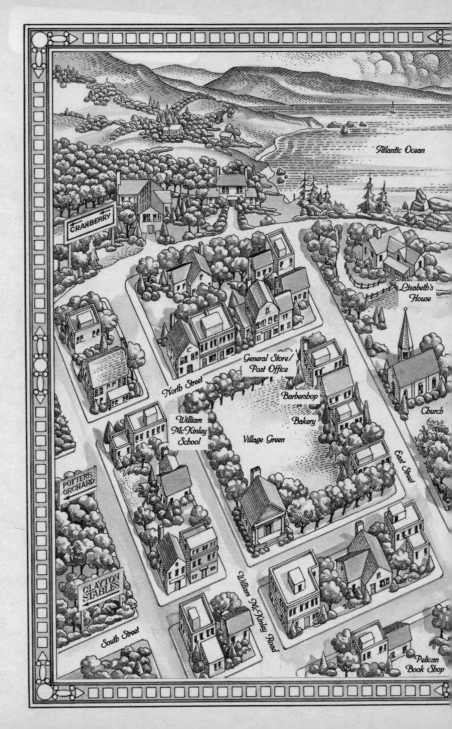

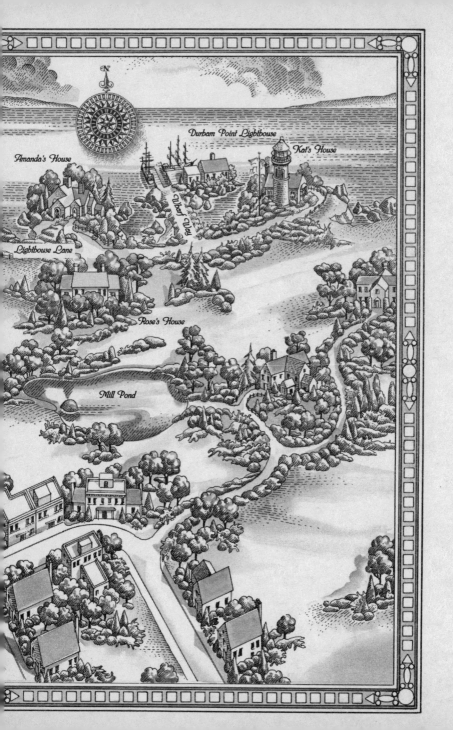

THOMAS KINKADE

The Girls of Lighthouse Lane

Lizabeth's Story

A CAPE LIGHT NOVEL

By Erika Tamar

SCHOLASTIC INC.

New York   Toronto   London   Auckland   Sydney
Mexico City   New Delhi   Hong Kong   Buenos Aires

ISBN 0-439-80669-0

Copyright © 2004 by Thomas Kinkade, The Thomas Kinkade Company,
Morgan Hill, CA, and Parachute Publishing, L.L.C.
Map of Cape Light by Joseph Scrofani. All rights reserved.
Published by Scholastic Inc., 557 Broadway, New York, NY 10012,
by arrangement with HarperCollins Publishers. SCHOLASTIC and
associated logos are trademarks and/or registered trademarks of Scholastic Inc.

12 11 10 9 8 7 6 5 4 3 2   5 6 7 8 9 10/0

Printed in the U.S.A.   40

First Scholastic printing, November 2005

The Girls of Lighthouse Lane

Lizabeth's Story

✥one✥

"**I** can't wait to show you my new dress!" Lizabeth Merchant said. It was all she could do to keep from clapping her hands with pleasure. "The dressmaker just finished it yesterday."

Kat, Amanda, Rose, and Lizabeth were walking home from school along William McKinley Road. The sidewalk wasn't wide enough for the four girls to walk side by side. Lizabeth walked backward in front of the others. Her elbow grazed the azaleas along the sidewalk.

"And wait till you see the color—strawberry!" Lizabeth continued.

"Strawberry?" Amanda asked. "You mean red?"

"Sort of dark pink. I'm hoping it will make the judges think of strawberries. So then they'll automatically picture me as the Strawberry Queen."

"If you really want to look like a strawberry," Kat said, "you should wear a pointed green cap."

Kat's grin was contagious and Lizabeth laughed in spite of herself. "Oh, stop!"

"Anyway, Lizabeth, you're allergic to strawberries," Kat said.

The trouble with cousins, Lizabeth thought, was that they knew all about you, even your allergies. But why did Kat have to remind her of her hives! "I wasn't planning to *eat* them," Lizabeth said.

"They might expect the queen to have at least a bite of strawberry shortcake, don't you think?" Amanda said.

"Remember last year?" Lizabeth asked. "The beauty event was in the evening, much later than the rest of the Strawberry Festival. The afternoon in the churchyard was separate. That's when they had the strawberry shortcake, strawberries and cream—"

"Strawberry-and-rhubarb pie," Kat interrupted. "Yum!"

"I *know* they gave the queen some strawberries right after the crowning," Amanda said. "To make the point, I guess."

"What point?"

"That strawberries are good."

"Oh." Lizabeth frowned. "I suppose I could *pretend* to eat them. And . . . and then drop them in my handkerchief!" If there would be no way around it, she thought, she'd have to swallow one or two. The hives wouldn't show up until later, and being Strawberry Queen was worth a little itching. Well, even a *lot* of itching.

"What beauty event?" Rose looked confused. "Why are we talking about strawberries?"

"Oh, you don't know about the Strawberry Festival, do you?" Lizabeth said. Rose Forbes had just moved to Cape Light in March and they still had to explain many of the town's traditions to her. "It's always in May. Anyone over thirteen from Cape Light or Cranberry can compete for Strawberry Queen. And I turned thirteen in January, so it's my first chance. May nineteenth, 1906! Only eleven days away!"

"Rose, I can't believe you've lived here for only two months," Kat said. "It feels like we've all been friends forever and ever."

Rose gave a quick, pleased smile. The smile lit up Rose's face and made her close to beautiful, Lizabeth thought, but she wasn't serious competition for Strawberry Queen. Rose had that striking coloring—blue-black hair and ivory skin—but she was too thin and tall, and not very graceful. Except on horseback. She was always coming or going from her uncle Ned's stables, with bits of hay stuck to her clothes or in her hair.

"Strawberry Festival is about celebrating Cape Light's bumper crop of strawberries," Amanda explained.

Rose smiled. "And I bet the town of Cranberry gets a bumper crop of—*cranberries!*"

Kat nodded. "The cranberry bogs were there long before the high school and the town hall were built."

"Anyway, all the women bring their best strawberry dishes and sell them," Amanda continued. "The profits go to needy families. It's fun and it's for a good cause."

Lizabeth studied Amanda. Her eyelashes were throwing long shadows on her cheeks. They were *unbelievably* long! Amanda's hair was ordinary light brown, while Lizabeth had lovely blond curls. And Amanda's complexion was pale, not peaches-and-cream like Lizabeth's. But Amanda had perfect, delicate features. Many people said she was the prettiest girl in Cape Light.

"Um . . . Amanda? Are you entering the Strawberry Queen event?" Lizabeth asked.

"Me? Oh, no," Amanda said.

Whew, Lizabeth thought, that's a relief! But then, almost against her will, she said, "You ought to. You'd probably win."

Amanda shook her head. "Father wouldn't like it."

"You worry too much," Lizabeth said. She was sure Reverend Morgan didn't disapprove of nearly as many things as Amanda feared. He was friends with Rose's parents, even though her mother was a *suffragette*.

Amanda shrugged. "I wouldn't be comfortable."

"How about you, Rose?" Lizabeth asked.

Rose shook her head. "I'm not that brave."

Maybe Rose knows she doesn't have a chance at Strawberry Queen, Lizabeth thought.

"How about you, Kat?" Lizabeth asked—though Kat had freckles to go with her flyaway auburn hair. She had a pretty, lively face, but she didn't take care of herself. She went out in the sun and didn't give a hoot for using a parasol!

Kat shrugged. "I don't think so."

"But the Strawberry Queen gets to ride in the mayor's carriage for the Fourth of July parade and everyone cheers her!"

"Sorry, it all sounds silly to me." Kat smiled. "You've got a clear field, Lizabeth. We'll all go to see you win."

Lizabeth bit her lip. "Do you really think I have a chance?"

"You can win over any girl in Cape Light." Kat laughed. "Especially if you look like a strawberry!"

Hmm, Lizabeth thought, but what about the Cranberry girls? "That Cranberry girl won last year. Claire Piedmont. She *is* awfully pretty but—" Lizabeth lowered her voice "—everyone knows she's *fast*."

"How do you know?" Amanda asked. "You shouldn't say that about anyone."

"You always like to think the best of everyone, but it was all over town. She was seen coming from the Potters' barn with my brother, Christopher."

"That doesn't mean anything," Rose said.

"Yes it does," Lizabeth said. "I hate to talk about my own brother, but Chris is getting a reputation for being wild. He courted Dorothy Lane for about ten minutes last year and then Claire Piedmont. Well, that wasn't even *courting*. And he's supposed to be apprenticing at the bank with my father after school, but no one can ever find him."

"Just because Chris doesn't like the bank, that doesn't make him wild," Rose said. Two pink spots had appeared on her cheeks. "And those girls . . . that was last year, wasn't it? When he was still fourteen and not serious about anything."

Lizabeth stared at Rose. She hardly knew Chris, so what was that all about?

"Anyway, I don't think Claire Piedmont can win

twice, do you?" Lizabeth said. "Let's see, today's the eighth. I have my matching ribbon and my shoes all ready. I guess I'm all set except for my last-minute beauty secrets."

"Wait a minute! Is it already the eighth?" Kat said. "Oh no! MY report is due tomorrow! Why did Miss Cotter have to give us a big assignment at the very end of the term?"

"Native cultures is an interesting topic," Lizabeth said.

"But it's just when we think we're through with school," Amanda said.

"School in Cape Light finishes so early," Rose said. "In New York it went on to the end of June."

"A lot of our classmates have to help with the spring chores. Farmwork and getting the fishing boats shipshape," Kat explained.

"My report is due tomorrow, too," Lizabeth said. "It's almost done. I ordered a book about the Aborigines of Australia from the Pelican Book Shop and it came in last week. I didn't think there'd even be one!"

Kat sighed. "All I know about Eskimos is what I found in the school encyclopedia: one paragraph."

"I'm supposed to do Pygmies and I found exactly

one sentence in the encyclopedia. All I know is they're short," Amanda complained. "Well, my report isn't due until Friday."

"Gosh, I wish I had thought . . . I'm sorry," Lizabeth said. "I could have ordered books for everyone from the Pelican Book Shop. Maybe I still can."

Lizabeth liked to help out her best friends. Kat's father was the lighthouse keeper and Amanda's father was the minister, and they couldn't afford anything extra. Rose was well-off, Lizabeth thought. Her father was the new doctor from New York City and her mother was very fashionable. Still no one in town was as rich as the Merchants.

"No, it's too late to order anything," Kat said. "Anyway, it's our own fault. We could have gone to the library in Cranberry."

Library books are handled by *strangers*, Lizabeth thought. And they might have just picked their noses!

Kat sighed. "We'll have to listen to five reports every day for the whole week, until everyone's had a turn. It'll be *endless*!"

"I think it'll be interesting. The Aborigines certainly are," Lizabeth said. "They have a tradition called the walkabout. It's a challenge for boys when they come of age. I don't know about the girls—the book didn't say. And grown men walkabout, too, when they're troubled."

"What's a walkabout?" Rose asked.

"The book said it's to find your true self, but I don't really know what that means," Lizabeth said. "You start walking all alone in the outback—that's a very harsh desert. You leave all your possessions behind. You don't take *anything*, not a single thing. Can you imagine? *My* true self would want an extra dress and at least a hairbrush! And some cologne would be nice if I can't take a bath for a while."

Kat grinned. "I don't think you'll be going on a walkabout anytime soon."

Lizabeth laughed. "No, I wouldn't think so!"

"It must be hard to survive without anything at all," Rose said.

"The journey is supposed to go on until you meet yourself," Lizabeth said. "It could be very long."

"You meet yourself?" Amanda asked.

"It's meant to be spiritual, I think," Lizabeth said. "Does it sound something like Moses or Jesus in the wilderness?"

"You could ask my father about that," Amanda said.

Lizabeth nodded. "I think I will."

"Lizabeth, watch out!" Kat said.

"What?"

"You're about to smash Mrs. Alveira's tulips!"

Lizabeth glanced over her shoulder. "Oops." She just missed stepping on the bright yellow flowers. Walking backward wasn't that easy.

"I'm glad I was assigned Indians," Rose said. "The Cherokee were brilliant at training horses. The horses were left behind by the Spanish conquistadors and—"

Amanda laughed. "Your report is supposed to be about the Indians, not their *horses*!"

"But horses were a big part of their culture." Rose looked around at the other girls. "Well, they were! Honest, I'm not making that up."

Lizabeth smiled and shook her head. Rose was horse-crazy for sure. If she wasn't at Clayton Stables or riding her own horse, Midnight Star, she found some way to bring horses into whatever else she was doing.

"I thought you were going to research the local Indians. The Cape Cod Indians," Amanda said.

"That was the Nauset tribe," Rose said. "It was too hard to find information. They became extinct in the 1600s because of an epidemic that came here with European seamen. Anyway, it was too sad."

"What kind of epidemic?" Lizabeth asked.

"The book said it was most probably smallpox," Rose said. "We're lucky there's a smallpox vaccination now."

"What's lucky about it? I think it's terrible that Massachusetts law forces everyone to get vaccinated," Lizabeth complained. "Look. It gave me this scar." She hated the indented mark near her shoulder. Except for that her skin was so perfectly smooth.

"It doesn't even show," Kat said. "And you're not making sense. Smallpox left people with *awful* scars, if it didn't kill them first! Whoever invented the vaccine was a hero."

"It was Edward Jenner. My father prays someone will discover ones for diphtheria and scarlet fever and cholera and everything else," Rose said.

"Lizabeth, watch out," Kat warned.

"What? More tulips?" Lizabeth said.

"It's Crazy Mary!" Amanda gasped.

Lizabeth whirled around. Crazy Mary was two steps away from her at the side of the road. Lizabeth could smell her. *Whew*! She'd almost bumped into Crazy Mary!

Kat, Amanda, and Rose crossed to the other side of the street and Lizabeth rushed after them. They made a wide circle around the ragged woman as they continued on their way.

"Do you see what she's doing?" Rose said.

Lizabeth took a wary glance back. Crazy Mary was on her knees. Her long gray hair streamed down her back. She was grunting and pulling up the blue and white flowers at the side of the road. Her face was bunched up with fury.

"Those are the Whites' irises!" Kat stopped. "Should we say something?"

"No, don't." Lizabeth held Kat's sleeve. "Don't talk to her."

"But—" Kat started.

"Come on, she's too scary." Lizabeth tugged at Kat. "Come on, let's keep walking."

"Anyway, she's stopped pulling flowers," Rose said. "Now she's scratching her backside!"

"She's looking right at us!" Lizabeth said. Crazy Mary was glaring at them. "Come on!"

"Pa says she's harmless," Kat said.

"He can't know that for sure," Lizabeth said. "She could attack somebody!"

The girls walked faster. This time, Lizabeth faced front. She wasn't taking any chance of bumping into something horrid.

⊱ *two* ⊰

The girls turned onto North Street. The great old trees edging the village green shaded the pavement and threw leafy patterns on their faces. The statue of the lost fisherman in the middle of the square of lawn was spotlighted by rays of afternoon sunlight.

They cut across the lawn toward Lizabeth's home on Lighthouse Lane.

There were masses of pink and orange azaleas in front of the large, white brick house. The trellis curving over the front path was covered with rose branches. There were already buds on the side trellis. The railing around the front porch was freshly painted and sparkling white.

"Hello! I'm home, Ada," Lizabeth called.

She led the other girls past the coat stand and through the front hall. They walked around the small mahogany table with its silver tray for calling cards, and past the forest green velvet hall chair.

"Is Mother here?" Lizabeth asked.

Above the chair rail, the walls were hand-stenciled with big scarlet roses and dark-green leaves. Peacock feathers were displayed in a floor vase at the foot of the curving white staircase. The hall smelled of beeswax floor polish.

"No, your mother went to the ladies' auxiliary tea. She'll be gone until dinner." Ada, the cook, came out of the back hall door under the stairs. She tucked a stray wisp of gray-blond hair into her bun and wiped a hand on the apron that strained to cover her roly-poly body. "Hello, Lizabeth, girls. What would you like for refreshments? I have some scones cooling off and there's strawberry jam for everyone else—apple jelly for you, Lizzie."

A frown crossed Lizabeth's face. How many times had she told Ada *never* to call her Lizzie! It was certainly improper for a servant even if Ada had practically raised her.

"No thank you, Ada. Nothing for me," Kat said. She turned to Lizabeth. "I can only stay a minute. That Eskimo report! And it's my turn to mop up before my lighthouse shift."

"Oh. All right," Lizabeth said. Kat had so many chores to do, along with her lighthouse watch every evening. And that was on top of the gift paper she designed and painted and sold to the local stores for spending money. It was hard to believe that their mothers were sisters. Marrying a rich man made all the difference.

The cinnamon-and-spice aroma of freshly baked scones followed them up the winding staircase.

They entered Lizabeth's lavender-and-white bedroom. The casement windows were open and crisp white organdy curtains fluttered in the spring breeze.

"Sorry for the mess." Lizabeth shrugged. "I guess the maid didn't get upstairs today." She halfheartedly picked up some unmentionables and discarded shirt-waists from the lavender rug.

"You can't just drop things on the floor." Amanda started to tidy up. "Lizabeth, you're a clutter-bug!"

"Never mind about that." Lizabeth opened her closet with a flourish. "Here it is!"

"Hello!" The door of the room suddenly flew open and four-year-old Tracy bounced into the room.

Amanda and Rose greeted her, and Kat tousled her little cousin's curly blond hair. Lizabeth muttered, "You're supposed to *knock*!"

"What are you doing?" Tracy asked.

"Nothing," Lizabeth said.

"Can I play, too?" Tracy asked.

"We're not *playing* anything." Lizabeth exhaled with exasperation.

Amanda smiled at the little girl. "Maybe later," she said.

Lizabeth took the strawberry dress out of the closet. Tissue paper was stuffed in its sleeves and under the skirt.

"Mother bought the fabric in Boston," Lizabeth said, "but it originally came all the way from *France*." She twisted the hanger and the silk pleats of the long skirt twirled, shading from deep pink to red.

"Oooh, it's lovely," Rose breathed.

"It is," Kat added. "You'll look beautiful!"

"See the tucks on the bodice? And that tiny bit of lace crochet around the neckline?" Lizabeth said. "The dressmaker wanted to—"

"Hello, Rose Lorraine Forbes," Tracy interrupted, chanting. "Hello, Katherine Lee Williams—"

"The dressmaker wanted to—"

"Hello, Amanda Jane Morgan," Tracy continued.

"For goodness' sake!" Lizabeth said. "We *know* you know everyone's names! Anyway, the dressmaker wanted to—"

"But I know all the *middle* names, too," Tracy said.

"Lizabeth Julia Merchant. Tracy Delia Merchant. Tracy is for Mother's grandfather Edward B. Tracy but—"

"Stop showing off, Tracy," Lizabeth said. "We're trying to talk."

"You were saying the dressmaker wanted . . ." Amanda prompted.

"—but when I start school," Tracy chattered on, "I'm telling everyone to call me Delia."

Lizabeth shook her head. "I completely forgot what I was about to say!"

"Try it on!" Rose said. "Let's see it on you."

"I would, but I'm afraid to wrinkle it," Lizabeth said. "I don't think I should take the tissue out yet; I have to keep it perfect for the festival." She replaced the dress in her closet carefully. She shoved other dresses out of the way to make plenty of room so that it wouldn't be crushed.

"No one's going to look prettier," Kat said. "I bet anything you'll be Strawberry Queen."

Tracy clapped her hands. "Are you going to be Strawberry Queen?"

"I don't know." Lizabeth picked a pale turquoise dress embroidered with pink and green sprigs out of her closet. "Kat, I love this color on you. Do you want it?"

Amanda's clothes came from the Sears Roebuck catalog, not even fitted to her. But even worse, Kat's clothes were sewn by her mother! If a bolt of fabric at the general store was reduced in price, chances are Kat would soon be wearing a dress of that very material.

"No, thanks," Kat said. "It's beautiful, but I don't have any occasion."

"You *do*! If you change your mind and enter for Strawberry Queen," Lizabeth said. The pale turquoise would be perfect with Kat's flaming red hair.

Kat smiled. "Thanks, but I don't care about a beauty contest. Honest. Now if you ever hear of an *art* contest, that's what I'd want to enter!"

"You'd win *any* art competition," Lizabeth said.

"Who's going to be Strawberry Queen?" Tracy asked.

"I don't know!" Tracy could try anyone's patience, Lizabeth thought. "Why don't you go play in your room and let us talk."

"Because I have nothing to *dooooo*." Tracy whined the last word.

"Ask Ada to read to you."

"No." Tracy sat down on Lizabeth's four poster bed and firmly planted herself on the quilt. It was mostly white, with scattered bunches of violets. "I want to play with *you*! And Rose Lorraine and Katherine Lee and Amanda Jane."

"Later," Amanda whispered.

"How are you wearing your hair?" Rose asked.

"Pompadour on top and curls in the back. I'll try to make sausage curls with Mother's curling iron and I'll put them up with an extra-long matching ribbon." Lizabeth had a clear image of her blond curls caught by the pink velvet ribbon, its ends trailing down. "It was almost impossible to find a match. I looked everywhere, and Mother finally found it in a shop in Cranberry. Let me show you. I think it's the exact color."

Lizabeth opened the shallow top drawer of her dresser and gasped. Instead of her neatly rolled-up ribbons—of grosgrain and satin, in rainbow colors to match her clothes—there was a messy jumble. The white ones were mixed up with the blues, and some were badly wrinkled. And no sign of strawberry pink velvet!

Lizabeth whirled around. "Tracy! You were in my ribbon drawer again!"

Tracy's eyes widened. "I . . . I didn't hurt anything." Her voice became very thin. "I . . . I didn't."

"How many times do I gave to tell you! *Keep out of my drawer!*"

"I only wanted to . . . The way you fixed my hair yesterday with a pretty ribbon. I wanted to—"

"I need a lock for my door!" Lizabeth's voice rose with her anger.

The little girl popped her thumb into her mouth.

"I need a lock for every drawer. Anything to keep you out! And get your thumb out of your mouth. It looks too stupid!"

Tracy's eyes welled up. She removed her thumb and clenched her hands together tightly.

"Lizabeth, it's only a bunch of ribbons," Kat said.

"The strawberry velvet ribbon is *missing* and I planned my whole outfit . . . " Lizabeth stared at Tracy. "Where is it?"

"I . . . I don't know," Tracy whimpered.

"Do you have it?"

Tracy shook her head.

"Oh, what's the use! Tracy, just *go*. Go away!"

Everyone could see that Tracy was holding back tears. Her whole face crumpled as she left the room.

"You're too hard on her," Amanda said. "You forget she's only four years old."

Lizabeth sighed. "Well, I have to do *something* to keep her out of my things."

"She wants to be just like her big sister," Kat said. "That's why she gets into your things."

"Even though Hannah's older," Amanda said, "I would never be that harsh with my little sister."

"That's different," Lizabeth said. Poor Hannah depended on Amanda for everything since their mother died in childbirth. It was completely different. "Tracy has to learn to respect my property. She really is spoiled."

"She seems extra-bright," Rose said. "And she's so cute."

"You don't know, Rose," Lizabeth said. "It's a lot easier to be an only child like you."

"Well, I think Tracy is adorable," Rose said. "And I think your brother, Chris, is wonderful!"

Lizabeth raised her eyebrows. "You think *my brother* is *wonderful*?"

Rose's face had taken on a pink glow.

"I thought you met him only once—the day I introduced you at the railroad station," Lizabeth said. Chris didn't go to the William McKinley grade school with them; he went to the high school in Cranberry. How would Rose know anything about him?

"He comes to my uncle's stables pretty often," Rose said. "A lot of afternoons. And we talk."

"Chris is interested in *riding*?" That was the first Lizabeth had heard of it!

"He is . . . now. He's getting very good at it." Rose ducked her head down a little. "But . . . I think he comes to see me."

"What's going on? Do you *like* him?" Lizabeth asked.

"Oh, I do! He's nice and interesting and—" Rose's words came out in an enthusiastic rush. "He's charming, and he makes me laugh, and we have so much to talk about!"

One of the things Lizabeth liked most about Rose was that she was completely straightforward. Most girls would pretend to be disinterested, but Rose didn't seem to know how. Just this once, Lizabeth thought, she wished Rose could pretend. Rose wasn't Chris's sort at all. He had an eye for much flashier, flirtier girls—and they certainly had an eye for him! Lizabeth's heart sank. Rose was going to get hurt. And then Rose would be embarrassed when she remembered admitting she liked Chris. Just thinking about it made Lizabeth furious at her brother.

"Well, Christopher and Tracy could both disappear, as far as I'm concerned!" Lizabeth said.

She caught Kat's disapproving look. Of course she didn't *mean* it, Lizabeth thought. Kat had to know she loved Chris and most especially little Tracy. For goodness' sake, it was only words!

~three~

izabeth was lucky she'd had a late tea of Ada's scones. Father came home late from the bank, so dinner wasn't served until half past seven.

Father placed the white linen napkin on his lap with an angry gesture. "I was kept waiting all evening for a telegram from that banker in New York! What's *wrong* with those people?"

He was in a terrible mood. Lizabeth was sure that hunger was adding to Father's irritation because he certainly had a strong appetite. He still cut a fine figure, though the gold buttons of his waistcoat threatened to pop over his well-rounded stomach. He was the very picture of prosperity, a man who could enjoy a whole roast goose and then afford to soothe his liver with trips to the mineral springs at Saratoga.

"Incompetent fools," Father grumbled.

"Now, now, Stanton . . ." Mother patted his arm.

Ada served the cream of mushroom soup and tip-toed out of the room.

They ate hungrily, silver spoons clanking against china bowls. All except Tracy, who had pushed her soup away untouched. She slumped over the table.

"Sit up straight, Tracy," Father said.

Tracy moved so slowly that Lizabeth was afraid Father would take it as disobedience. Father had no patience with Tracy. Though she was a bright, enchanting little imp, with deep dimples and huge navy blue eyes, Father said he had no interest in nursery twaddle. He said children didn't interest him until they were twelve or so and could hold a decent conversation.

"Can't anyone teach the child to keep her elbows off the table?" Father growled.

If Tracy was yelled at twice in one day, that would be too much. Maybe I was a little too hard on her, Lizabeth thought.

"I know you had a difficult day at the bank, Stanton, but please try to relax," Mother said. "For the sake of your digestion, dear."

But Father turned to Chris. "Perhaps if you had managed to honor us with your presence this afternoon."

Chris's face froze. "I'm sorry, sir. I never said I'd be

coming in to the bank."

"What does that mean?" Father was bristling with anger now. "You've been handed a golden opportunity that other boys would be more than grateful for!"

"I suppose . . . if that's what they want." Chris kept his tone polite, but his rebellious eyes gave him away. "But I don't."

Ada brought in the main course, interrupting at just the right time to avoid a scene between Father and Chris. Father didn't believe in airing the family laundry in front of the hired help.

Lizabeth glanced over at her sister. Tracy was unusually quiet. Still sulking, Lizabeth thought. Well, Lizabeth refused to feel guilty! Tracy had deserved getting yelled at, hadn't she? But normally, Tracy bounced back in no time at all. . . .

Tracy was pushing mashed potatoes around her plate without bringing any to her lips. Lizabeth was glad Father didn't notice. He never allowed them to play with their food.

Ada served the crystal bowls of butterscotch pudding and cleared her throat. "Excuse me, sir? Ma'am?"

"Yes, Ada."

"If I could leave now, please, with dinner so late and

all. You see, my sister Leda is feeling poorly and I promised I'd stop by and give supper to the children."

"Leda?" Mother asked. "Is she the one who cooks for Dr. and Mrs. Forbes?"

"No, ma'am, that's Edna. Leda is the youngest of us, with three little ones. She's taken to bed and I said I'd help out with the children tonight."

"All right, Ada, go ahead," Mother said.

"Thank you, ma'am, I'll just pour the coffee and—"

Tracy pushed her pudding away. "I don't want any."

"But butterscotch is your very favorite!" Ada exclaimed. "I made it especially for you."

"I don't feel so good," Tracy whispered.

Tracy must have stuffed herself with Ada's scones all afternoon, Lizabeth thought.

"Oh, dear," Ada said. "Does something hurt?"

Tracy's head sagged onto the table. "I feel sick."

"Sit up, dear. Let me see." Mother put her hand on Tracy's forehead. "She feels a little warm. Maybe a cold coming on. Do you want to go up to bed, sweetheart?"

Tracy nodded.

"All right, run along. I'll come up soon."

Ada's worried eyes followed Tracy. "I think we should call Dr. Forbes, ma'am. I mean, if she's feverish. . . ."

"I said she felt a little warm, that's all," Mother said. "That doesn't mean *feverish*. I don't think we need the doctor for every little sniffle."

"She didn't eat a thing," Ada said. "And she's *never* so quiet."

"That's enough, Ada." Father didn't like it when Ada took over Mother's role. Ada did that more than he knew, Lizabeth thought, especially with Tracy. You'd think the sun rose and set with Tracy!

"You go ahead and take care of your responsibilities," Father continued.

Ada was practically wringing her hands. "But, sir, I can't help worrying. . . ."

"We appreciate that, Ada," he said more kindly. "We'll watch her and we'll certainly call Dr. Forbes if necessary."

Ada nodded. "Yes, sir."

Chris got up from the table. "I'd like to be excused, too."

Father scowled, but then Mother said, "Let him go, Stanton. It's almost nine."

"Me too." Lizabeth scooped the last bit of pudding from her bowl. "May I be excused? I have to go to Amanda's."

"It's awfully late to visit her," Mother said.

"Well, it's not really to see Amanda," Lizabeth explained. "I want to ask Reverend Morgan about walk-abouts. About the spiritual side of them."

"Walk what?" Father asked.

"The journey that Aborigines take to . . . um . . . meet themselves."

"What are you *talking* about, Lizabeth?" Father asked. He didn't wait for an answer. "The point is to expand the bank," he told Mother, "and those people should see there's money to be made!"

Lizabeth's chair scraped against the shining parquet floor as she stood up.

"Do you have to go right *now*, Lizabeth?" Mother asked. "At this hour?"

"It's for my end-term report. And Amanda said her father comes home around nine."

"That man is a saint," Mother said. "I hear he's out till all hours counseling anyone who needs him—church members or not. But aren't his girls often left alone late into the evening?"

Lizabeth nodded. "I think Amanda wishes he wasn't so busy with everyone else. But she says it's best to speak to troubled people when they're home from their days' work and relaxed after their dinner."

"That makes sense," Mother said. "He's certainly selfless."

"It would be lots better for Amanda if he wasn't so selfless," Lizabeth said. "I feel funny about taking more of his time, but Amanda told me to come. She said nothing pleases him more than discussing spiritual questions with young people."

"Don't stay too long," Father said.

"I won't. Good night, Father. Good night, Mother."

Lizabeth walked out and across the wide front porch. The shape of a man was silhouetted by the gas lamp on the path and for a moment Lizabeth was startled. Then she saw that it was Christopher leaning against the railing. She thought he had gone upstairs to his room.

"What are you doing?" she asked.

"Breathing."

"Mmm, I know." She inhaled deeply. "May smells wonderful."

"That's not what I meant," Chris said. "I have to get out of the house to *breathe*."

"You shouldn't sass him, Chris. It wouldn't hurt to show up at the bank."

"Yes it would. I hate it."

"But you know you're going to take it over one day."

"No such thing!"

"I don't understand you," Lizabeth said. "Bankers make the most money."

Chris shrugged.

"There's another thing I don't understand," Lizabeth continued. She hesitated. She didn't know quite what to say, but if she could save Rose a lot of heartache . . . "About Rose. Why are you—"

"That's none of your business," Chris interrupted.

"Rose is my friend," Lizabeth said. "And I know she's not your sort at all—"

"And what's that supposed to mean?" Chris interrupted. "I'll tell you this much. She's not like everyone else. Rose doesn't think she's some porcelain doll. She'd never pretend to swoon or anything stupid like that, or act coquettish."

"She doesn't know how," Lizabeth muttered.

"When I see her ride Midnight Star, she amazes me!" Lizabeth was surprised by how enthusiastic Chris sounded. That wasn't like him at all.

"And she's not afraid to work and get dirty to keep the horses comfortable and fit," he continued. "Rose doesn't need to stop and primp either."

"You mean . . . she lets you watch her muck out the stall?" Lizabeth was astonished. She could just imagine Rose in that old cracked leather divided skirt of hers, with her hair tied back any which way, surrounded by the smell of manure instead of perfume! She was already fourteen, the oldest of their group, she should really know better! Someone has to talk to Rose about how to present herself in front of boys, Lizabeth thought.

"Sure. I help her with the stall sometimes," Chris was saying, "and scrubbing out the feed buckets and—"

"Well, that's the strangest way of courting I've ever heard of!"

"Who cares about *courting*?" Chris laughed. He put on that awful falsetto voice he used when he was being mean to her. "Courting is leaving your calling card on a silver tray in her front hall and calling her *Miss* Forbes and she calls you *Mister* Merchant and you take *proper* little walks and talk about nothing! It's not like that with me and Rose."

"You'd better be proper with her! She's my friend."

"She's my friend, too." Chris's eyes flared with anger. "You don't know a thing about it, so why don't you stop bothering me and go on your way?"

Lizabeth tossed her head and flounced down the

porch steps to the path. Christopher was impossible! She had planned to ask him to pick up a length of strawberry velvet ribbon in that shop in Cranberry. After all, it's near his school in Cranberry so it wouldn't be out of his way. But this didn't exactly seem to be the best time to ask him for a favor.

A boy was supposed to put a girl up on a pedestal. That's what everything she'd read in the *Ladies' Home Journal* and the Girls' Guides told her. She was supposed to be fragile and he was supposed to be inspired to romantic poetry by her feminine loveliness—certainly not by the way she communed with her horse! And there were occasions when swooning was exactly the right thing for a lady to do to show her delicacy. All those magazine articles couldn't possibly be wrong. It was right there in print!

four

"I agree with you, Lizabeth," Reverend Morgan was saying. "The Aborigines' walkabout in the desert does remind me somewhat of Moses and Jesus."

The worn leather armchair across the desk from Reverend Morgan was too big for Lizabeth, but she settled into it comfortably. His study, Lizabeth thought, was the one part of the house that didn't cry for a woman's touch. With crowded bookshelves on two walls, it looked exactly like what is was—the minister's place to work. The rest of Amanda's house seemed rather sad and lonely.

The minister's dark eyes radiated kindness, but he, too, had a sad and lonely air. "Moses wandered in the wilderness for forty days and forty nights to purify himself in preparation for receiving the Ten Commandments. And Jesus wandered alone in the wilderness, in much the same way, to prepare himself before he gave the Sermon on the Mount."

"But why do the Aborigines have to go without any food or possessions?" Lizabeth asked. "Their desert sounds terribly harsh."

"Yes, it does." Reverend Morgan's smile warmed his long, thin face. "Perhaps when you're hungry and tired and left to struggle on your own, all your defenses come down and you become open to recognizing some truths about yourself. Perhaps it's about stripping yourself bare, down to the basics, without the comfort of things you're used to, and depending only on yourself, without friends to help you. It forces you to come face-to-face with who you truly are."

"Coming face-to-face with who you truly are. . . ." Lizabeth was thoughtful. "Meeting yourself."

"Yes, that's what I think it means. Though as outsiders, we don't know all of the Aborigines' beliefs."

"Moses and Jesus wandered in the desert, too," Lizabeth said.

"It's not exactly the same, but I would say that all cultures reach out for the spiritual. That seems to be a human need. The Aborigines and our little congregation here in Cape Light aren't that different under the surface. In all the important ways, people are very much the same the world over."

"Then the whole world should be friendly," Lizabeth said.

"You know, I think you've just given me an idea for next Sunday's sermon!"

Lizabeth beamed with pleasure.

"The book I got from the Pelican Book Shop also shows pictures of Aboriginal art," she said. "They pass on their history through paintings instead of words. It's interesting, isn't it, Reverend Morgan?"

"Very interesting. I think you'll put together an excellent report, Lizabeth. Sounds like an A to me."

"Oh, I'm not using all of this in my report. I have enough already. I didn't mean to take up your time for no good reason. I just wanted to know for myself. But if I gave you an idea for a sermon, well, that makes me feel lots better!"

"Wanting to know for yourself is the most important thing," Reverend Morgan said. "Come back to talk anytime."

At school the next day, Miss Cotter announced, "Time for the native culture reports. Let's see . . . today we have Vernon, Mark, Katherine, Lizabeth, and Mabel. Well, no. Mabel is still out."

Mabel had been out last week, too. Lizabeth wondered if she was truly sick or helping out at her family's bait-and-tackle shop. Maybe she had a cold. Hannah had come to school with one. Her nose kept running and Amanda followed her around all day with a handkerchief.

"I have hardly anything," Kat whispered to Lizabeth. "And this morning Todd reminded me that he wrote about Eskimos for his book report last year. He turned in six pages! I just know Miss Cotter will compare us."

Kat's brother Todd was only ten, but he was one of the best students. Kat is never the least bit jealous, Lizabeth thought, and she always encourages him. It's nice for a brother and sister to be so close. It made Lizabeth feel a little sad.

"Kindergarten, grade one, and grade two in the back of the room, please, with Miss Harding," Miss Cotter said. The younger children grouped together for a reading lesson with Miss Harding, the assistant teacher. Grades three through nine sat in rows facing Miss Cotter.

"I hope I'm not in trouble," Kat whispered.

"Hurry and settle down," Miss Cotter said. "We'll start with Vernon."

Vernon shuffled to the front of the room. Poor

Vernon always had a bad time when he had to recite in front of the class.

"The Hottentots of . . . um . . . Africa," he mumbled.

"Speak up, Vernon," Miss Cotter said. "Everyone wants to hear you."

Vernon turned red and swiveled his body from side to side.

"The . . . um . . . Hottentots . . . are a tribe in . . . uh . . . Africa." Lizabeth could see the pages shaking in his hand. He mumbled and stumbled his way through a lengthy report. It might be excellent, Lizabeth thought, but it was too hard to listen to him.

Then came Mark. "The Bedouins of Arabia. They wear blue robes and they're nomads and live in tents in the desert. They eat sheep's eyes."

All the girls said, "Eeeww," and got a stern look from Miss Cotter.

When he came to the camels, Mark became passionate. "Camels are perfect for the desert because they can store water for a long time. People say they smell bad, and they spit when they're mad, but I think they should be appreciated. The Bedouins would be nowhere without their camels. They do everything our horses do and even more. There are camels and dromedaries, one hump and two, and—" He went on and on, telling more about camels than anyone would ever want to know, Lizabeth thought. She chuckled to herself. Mark was the blacksmith's son. Maybe he hoped to shoe all those camels!

A loud, high voice came from the back of the room. "See Jane run!" Then a "shhh-shhh" from Miss Harding and the younger children's reading lesson settled into a background murmur again.

Kat was next. "The Eskimos. The Eskimos don't go out to sea the way Cape Light fishermen do. The sea is frozen where they live, and they make holes in the ice and catch seals and things like that. They live in igloos made of blocks of ice, and they eat blubber—that's animal fat—and that helps keep them warm in their cold climate." Kat stopped speaking.

Miss Cotter raised her eyebrows. "Go on."

"The end," Kat whispered.

Lizabeth had an awful feeling that Miss Cotter was about to reprimand Kat. At least Miss Cotter was fair, not like Miss Harding, who liked to rap knuckles with her ruler for any little thing.

"Now really, Katherine," Miss Cotter said. "I'd think you, of all people, could tell us about Eskimo art and the ivory carvings they make."

"Oh," Kat said. "I didn't know about that."

"You certainly made no effort," Miss Cotter said. "Your report was . . ." She shook her head. "I can hardly give you any grade at all."

"Miss Cotter, I have something else." Kat unfurled a spectacular watercolor painting. It showed an Eskimo man and a little boy fishing through a hole in a vast expanse of ice. It was white upon white upon white, ice and snow and white clouds in a gray-white winter sky. The ice gleamed and you could become chilled just from looking at it!

"Oh, my." Miss Cotter's frown disappeared. "We'll hang that in front of the classroom!"

Kat's talent always made Lizabeth proud that they were related.

"Now, Lizabeth. Are you ready?"

"Yes, Miss Cotter." Lizabeth walked to the front of the room and cleared her throat. "The Aborigines. The Aborigines live in Australia in the part called the outback. It's mostly desert and very harsh. It's hot as a furnace in the dry season and there are terrible rains in the wet season." Lizabeth read a few more paragraphs about Australia, the Aborigines, and the animals in the outback. Her report was just long enough to avoid criticism from Miss Cotter.

～ ⚘ ～

"I was looking forward to your report," Rose said. The girls had gathered in the tower of the lighthouse after school. "I was surprised it was so short. I thought you'd say much more."

"Me, too," Kat said. "You left out the walkabout."

"My father was impressed," Amanda added. "He said you were so interested and had done loads of reading."

"Well . . . yes," Lizabeth said. "But it wasn't for the report. I was curious. I just wanted to know."

"I don't get it," Kat said. "If you already did the reading, why didn't you . . . you're not suddenly getting as shy as poor Vernon, are you?"

Amanda laughed. "Our Lizabeth? Never!"

"Well, then why?" Kat asked again.

"It's simple, really." Lizabeth leaned back against the wide windowsill. It held a kerosene lantern, lengths of rope, tools, and some of Kat's seascapes. "It's very useful for a girl to be smart, but not to *show* it."

"Oh, Lizabeth." Rose looked dismayed. "My mother says women should be working extra-hard to prove we're as smart as anybody. We could be doctors or

41

lawyers or anything."

"Your mother is nice as can be, but she *is* a suffragette." Mrs. Forbes was beautiful and charming, but she was one of those bloomer girls, always arguing for the vote for women. Rose seemed to be picking up some of her odd beliefs. Lizabeth shook her head. "Honestly, a woman doctor!"

"That would be peculiar," Amanda admitted.

"Who'd ever marry a woman who examines people's bodies? I'll bet women doctors—if there even are any—are all old maids," Lizabeth said. "It's really important to make a good match. Well, you know that's my main goal."

Rose frowned. "What does that have to do with your Aborigine report?"

"Everything! Men don't like girls who are too smart," Lizabeth explained. "That's quite off-putting to them. All the magazines say so."

"Don't tell me you want to make a match with one of the boys in our class!" Kat said.

"No, of course not!" Lizabeth laughed. "I do think Mark is rather handsome, but I'm not at all interested in blacksmiths!"

"If a boy is handsome and nice, it doesn't matter if

he's a blacksmith or—or a deckhand," Amanda said.

"You're thinking of that boy who stares at you in church, aren't you? Jed Langford?" Lizabeth asked.

"I try not to. My father says I can't have gentlemen callers until I'm at least fifteen. That's two whole years away!" Amanda looked so unhappy. "Jed won't keep liking me for two whole years, not if we can't even go walking together. We had only that one wonderful evening at the barn dance. And that was last October! He'll find someone else."

"A deckhand isn't suitable anyway," Lizabeth said.

"You're not as terrible a snob as you make yourself sound," Kat said.

"Nothing against Jed or Mark, but I'm being honest," Lizabeth said. "A girl has that one chance for a good life. Well, I'm thirteen now, so I'm *practicing* for later on, when it counts. And if I get to be Strawberry Queen, that should bring me a load of worthwhile suitors. Don't you think?"

Since the subject had come up already, Lizabeth was tempted to give Rose some advice. It was hard not to when a good friend didn't know how to act with boys. But she decided she'd better wait until they were alone. And she'd have to find a tactful way, without letting her know she had talked to Chris.

"Lizabeth, tell the truth now. . . ." Kat said.

"I always tell the truth, especially here in the tower."

"Last month, when you were two words away from winning the spelling bee—" Kat stopped. "Well, I was sure I remembered you practicing 'malevolence' ahead of time."

Lizabeth grinned and rattled off, "M-A-L-E-V-O-L-E-N-C-E."

Rose looked shocked. "Did you miss it on *pur-pose?*"

"Yes, I did. Being third runner-up is good enough," Lizabeth said. "The winner of the spelling bee—especially over two boys—that's the wrong kind of attention for a girl. But Strawberry Queen—now that's *positive* attention."

"We'll all be there cheering for you," Amanda said.

Suddenly there was loud barking from outside. It drowned out Amanda's soft voice.

"Is that Sunshine?" Rose asked. Sunshine was Kat's big white dog. He used to curl up next to them in the lighthouse tower, but he'd become too old to manage the two steep flights of stairs. Now he'd wait at the lighthouse door.

"Someone must be coming," Kat said.

The girls went to the windows. All they could see was miles of ocean and the treacherous rocks down below.

"Lizabeth! Come down, please!"

Lizabeth recognized her mother's voice. "I didn't know Mother would be visiting with Aunt Jean today," she said.

"It's still early for you to go home, isn't it?" Kat said.

"Well, as long as she's here with the carriage . . ." Lizabeth said. Odd that Mother hadn't said a thing this morning about stopping by.

"I should go, too," Amanda said. "I have to pick up Hannah from Mary Margaret's."

"We'll give you a ride," Lizabeth said. "You, too, Rose." Rose lived directly across Lighthouse Lane from Amanda, half a mile from the lighthouse on Durham Point.

Lizabeth, Kat, Rose, and Amanda hurried down the two flights from the tower. Their shoes clattered on the narrow stone steps.

Lizabeth's mother stood at the entrance to the lighthouse with Aunt Jean. She wore a hat and gloves—she'd never leave the house without them—and a perfectly nice afternoon suit, but she looked disheveled. Lizabeth stared at her. The jacket was buttoned wrong and twisted around her waist. Strands of hair were coming out of her pompadour and her hat looked as if it had been hastily slapped on. She was unusually pale and her eyes were full of anxiety. Aunt Jean, next to her, looked distressed, too.

Suddenly the sunny spring afternoon felt chilly and a bolt of fear rushed through Lizabeth.

"Mother, what's wrong?"

❧ *five* ❧

"It's Tracy." Mother's hand was at her mouth as if she wanted to hold back the words. "She has scarlet fever."

"Scarlet fever?" Lizabeth repeated.

"It will be all right. I know it will." Aunt Jean put her arm around Mother's shoulders. "The two Haley children in Cranberry came down with it, remember? In a week the fever broke and they were back to their normal mischief in no time."

Rose took Lizabeth's hand. "My father said almost everyone in Cranberry recovered."

"But some didn't," Mother whispered.

"Tracy has always been a strong, sturdy little girl, the picture of health," Aunt Jean said.

Mother took a deep, shuddering breath.

"She'll be fine," Aunt Jean said.

Lizabeth looked from her mother to Aunt Jean and

back again. Mother panics too easily, she thought. Tracy will be all right. People like us don't get *seriously* sick. That happens to poor people who don't have good food and nice, clean houses.

"We're in quarantine," Mother said.

"What do you mean quarantine?" Lizabeth asked.

"No one comes in or out of our house," Mother explained. "Dr. Forbes has to keep Cape Light from an epidemic. Strict quarantine, he said. No contact with anyone."

"Oh," Lizabeth said. It would be hard to be stuck at home but if it was only for a short time. . . . Didn't Aunt Jean just say the fever broke in a week? "All right, let's go home. I'll cheer up Tracy."

"Lizabeth, you don't understand. You *can't* come home." Mother's voice broke. "I can't have you exposed."

"But I have to go home. Where else—"

"I packed a suitcase for you," Mother interrupted. "It's in the carriage. You'll stay with your uncle Jasper and aunt Mavis in Pittsfield. I'm taking you right now."

"Not them!" Uncle Jasper was Father's eldest brother. Both he and Aunt Mavis were *ancient* and strict and gloomy! "Is Chris going there, too?"

"Chris is staying with Michael Potter in Cranberry.

He can't miss the last weeks of high school, all the tests and—"

"I can't miss the last week of school, either."

"Lizabeth, please don't make a fuss." Mother sounded exhausted. "I have to take you and get back to Tracy and—"

"Oh, the Strawberry Festival! I *can't* be in Pittsfield for the Strawberry Festival. It's May nineteenth!"

"Maybe Tracy will be well by then," Amanda said.

"I bet she will," Rose said.

Of course she will, Lizabeth thought. Scarlet fever wasn't *that* bad. Was it?

"Now wait a minute, Sue," Aunt Jean said. "Lizabeth will stay with us, of course. Why even think of sending her so far away?"

Kat nudged Lizabeth. "We'll have the best time!"

"I didn't want to trouble you. You don't have room for her," Mother said. "Jasper and Mavis have lots of extra space and—"

"Please, Mother," Lizabeth begged.

"Oh, pooh. It's not a bit of trouble," Aunt Jean said. "We'll put Lizabeth in Kat's room and the girls will have a lovely time. Now you just go ahead and take care of our darling Tracy until the roses are back in her cheeks."

"Thank you but . . . are you sure?" Mother asked.

"Not another word about it," Aunt Jean said.

"I suppose it could work out." Mother glanced at Lizabeth. "You'll have to help Aunt Jean and not get in the way. And—"

"I'll mind my manners and be ever so good." Lizabeth grinned at Kat. "And we won't get into any scrapes, will we?"

A week of sleeping over with Kat would be fun! Kat would help her get ready for the Strawberry Queen contest and she'd go there with the Williams family. If she won, that would cheer up Mother and Tracy and everybody.

"Lizabeth, come get your suitcase," Mother said. She turned to Aunt Jean. "Thank you. I have to rush right back. Stanton is holding down the fort at home and making arrangements to stay out of the bank for the week."

If Father is actually staying home from the bank, Lizabeth thought, that sounds *serious*. She brushed that terrible thought away. No, it's because Father will be in quarantine like everyone else. But even so, it wasn't right to look forward to staying with Kat when the reason was that her little sister was sick. She felt a chill of fear.

But God wouldn't let anything happen to Tracy. She

never hurt anyone or anything. Why, she even felt sorry
for the flowers when she picked them. . . .

At dinner, eight-year-old Jamie and Uncle Tom
moved over to make room at the round wood table.
Lizabeth was squeezed in between Kat and ten-year-old
Todd. Aunt Jean served a tureen of thick clam chowder
and coarse bread. Ironstone bowls were passed around.

Everyone helped themselves with the big soup
ladle.

"Jamie and I went clamming this afternoon," Todd
said proudly. "We got a big haul of quahogs down in the
eelgrass."

Lizabeth swallowed. *Eelgrass?*

"And clams are free!" Jamie sang out.

Kat shrugged. "Chowder with milk, chowder with
tomatoes, chowder with parsley . . . I get tired of it."

"It's a good, healthy Cape dish," Uncle Tom said.
"Though the only proper way is with milk and potatoes,
exactly like this. Anything else is criminal."

Lizabeth moved her spoon around her soup. It was
barely liquid, crammed with potatoes and heaven knew
what else. "It's very good, Aunt Jean," she said politely.
She hated thinking that the clams in her bowl had been

pulled out of eelgrass by Todd and Jamie. That sounded too slimy! How she longed for Ada's clear consommé with nothing more than a slice of lemon floating in it.

"Have some more, dear," Aunt Jean said. "You took hardly a spoonful."

"It's as thick and filling as a stew," Lizabeth answered cheerfully. "I'll have to leave room for the main course."

Jamie laughed. "This *is* the main course!"

Oops, Lizabeth thought.

"Hush, Jamie," Aunt Jean said. "Would you like something else, Lizabeth?"

"Oh, no. This is fine," Lizabeth said. She chewed and chewed on a lump of dark bread. She'd been at Kat's a million times, she thought, for a million after-school snacks. But she didn't remember ever actually having *dinner* here. For Thanksgiving and Christmas, the Williamses always came to the Merchants' house. There was so much more room at the Merchants' and of course, there was help, and it was just . . . *nicer*. True, no one was arguing or angry at the Williams table, and Kat's father joked and laughed a lot. Still, there was a lot to be said for crisp white tablecloths and linen napkins. Lizabeth sighed.

She felt Kat's sharp glance and quickly arranged a

pleasant expression on her face. She was awfully glad she was here and not in Pittsfield.

And now Aunt Jean was serving apple pie, still warm from the oven, with slices of cheddar. "That smells wonderful, Aunt Jean!" Lizabeth could certainly fill up on that.

After dinner Lizabeth and Kat went to the lighthouse for Kat's evening shift. They climbed up the ladder to the tower.

Lizabeth looked out of the windows all around the circular room. The ocean was crashing on the rocks below, sending sprays of white foam high into the air. The setting sun colored the waves orange and red.

"It's beautiful," Lizabeth said.

"It's different all the time," Kat said. "That's why I keep doing seascapes."

"Are you going to paint now?" Lizabeth asked. Kat would often paint here in the afternoons while Lizabeth, Amanda, and Rose talked. It was nice.

"No, it'll be too dark in a minute," Kat said.

"So turn on the light," Lizabeth said.

"Lizabeth, did you forget? The tower room only has the lantern."

"Oh." Lizabeth was used to electricity in every room.

The last of the sun's rays were sinking into the dark ocean.

"Well I'd better take care of it," Kat said. Kat took the lantern from the shelf. She trimmed the wick, filled it with kerosene, and lit it.

The lantern was reflected in the windows. Past the circle of brightness around it, the room became dim.

Lizabeth looked at the deep shadows on the stone floor. "I guess we can't play jacks either." It was strange how a place that was magical in the afternoon could become so uninviting when the sun went down. But she was determined to be cheerful.

"We can always talk." Lizabeth settled into a chair and smiled. "That's what we do most of the time anyway."

"I have some things to do first." Kat started up the second ladder that went high into the very top where the light was. Lizabeth remembered seeing the cramped space up there and she didn't like it at all. It was impossible to turn around without bumping into the stone walls.

"Do you want me to go with you?" Lizabeth asked. "Should I . . . um . . . help?" Help with *what*, she wondered. Anyway, there probably wasn't room for both of them up there.

"That's all right, I'll just be a minute," Kat called down as she disappeared.

"What are you doing?" Lizabeth called up to her.

"Winding the spring that makes the light revolve." Kat's voice bounced off the stone walls and took on an echo.

The light came on. Beyond its rays, everything was suddenly pitch black.

Kat climbed back down the ladder and picked up the shovel leaning against the coal stove.

"What are you doing now?"

"Ma always cleans out the ashes at the end of her morning watch. It's my job to stoke the new coals."

Lizabeth watched as Kat shoveled in lumps of coal. "That's too messy! Why do you have to do that, anyway? It's May!"

"It still gets cold up here at night." Kat wiped her hands off on a rag, but Lizabeth could see that they weren't really clean.

There's nothing like soap and running water, Lizabeth thought. She scooted her chair back out of touching range. But she suspected that coal dust was flying all around.

"What's the matter?" Kat asked.

"Nothing. Just that this is my new shirtwaist. . . ."

"Fancy white linen isn't the best thing to wear for a lighthouse shift," Kat said.

"When I got dressed this morning, how was I supposed to know I'd be stoking coals by nightfall?"

Kat raised her eyebrows. "You weren't exactly *stoking* it."

"Hmmm, that's true." Lizabeth had to laugh. "I guess I was *mentally* stoking it . . . to keep you company."

Kat laughed, too. "Oh, well. Thanks."

"Seriously, I'll help you with . . . whatever," Lizabeth said. She sat up straight, all set to get to work. "So now what?"

"Now we watch." Kat sat down next to Lizabeth and scanned the horizon. Lizabeth looked out the window, too. She watched the light revolve. Its rays covered miles in all directions. There wasn't a thing to see.

"You just *watch*?" Lizabeth yawned. "But nothing's happening."

"That's the point. We pray for nothing to happen," Kat said. "I'm on watch in case something does. We can talk, Lizabeth, but I'm supposed to be alert."

Lizabeth squirmed restlessly in her chair. "There aren't even any stars to look at."

"If I'd known you were coming, I'd have arranged for them to come out."

Lizabeth tapped her foot. "So you just sit here for hours, watching *nothing*?"

"What did you think a lighthouse shift was?" Kat's tone was sharp.

"Well, I didn't know," Lizabeth said. "It's boring." The tower room was their special place, but it wasn't much fun tonight. She stifled another yawn.

"If you're tired, you can turn in," Kat said. "You don't have to stay."

"It's too early to go to sleep," Lizabeth protested.

"Then go play with Todd and Jamie!"

"Are you mad, Kat? What are you mad about?"

"I'm not *mad*, but . . ." Kat sighed. "This is what I do and you don't have to act like it's so awful."

"I didn't say it was awful," Lizabeth said. "I just didn't know what a shift is like. I mean, it's different when we're here in the afternoon relaxing with Amanda and Rose. For goodness' sake, Kat, I was just *asking*."

"All right, I'm sorry I jumped on you," Kat said. "We can talk like we always do. The only difference is that I'm looking out the window."

Lizabeth didn't feel much like talking anymore. She

was busy thinking. How could she have forgotten, even for a minute, that the cottage had no running water? Tonight, she'd have to use the *outhouse*! And there was one bed—a narrow cot—in Kat's room. Where would she be sleeping? She hoped it wouldn't have to be on the floor!

❧ six ❧

Getting ready for bed was much harder here. There was the trip down the dark path to the outhouse. Kat carried a hurricane lamp to light their way. The bushes rustled and there was the constant buzz of insects. Lizabeth prayed she wouldn't have to go again during the night. There was a chamber pot in Kat's room, but who was supposed to empty it?

The girls had to carry water in from the well and heat it on the kitchen stove and carry it upstairs. Lizabeth started to give Kat a hand with the bucket.

"It's so *heavy*," Lizabeth said.

"That's okay," Kat said. "I've got it."

There was just enough water for one bath and it certainly wasn't the best bath Lizabeth had ever had! And then she felt guilty. She didn't realize.

"Sorry," Lizabeth said. "Did I use it all up? I didn't mean to."

"Don't worry," Kat said. "I'll take mine in the morning." She spread a bedroll on the floor. "You can have the bed."

"Are you sure?" Lizabeth asked halfheartedly.

"It's fine. I've slept on the bedroll lots of times."

Lizabeth wondered if she should offer to take the bedroll, but Kat didn't seem to mind. After her prayers, Kat tunneled comfortably under her quilt with Sunshine curled up next to her.

Lizabeth closed her eyes. She was used to smoothly ironed bed linens scented with lavender. Kat's sheets were coarse. The mattress was much thinner than hers at home—and lumpy. Whichever way she tossed and turned, she found new lumps. She thought of the story about the princess and the pea. Well, she wasn't a princess, but . . .

Lizabeth giggled. "Are you testing me, Kat?"

"What?" Kat mumbled sleepily.

"You didn't put a pea under the mattress, did you?"

"A pea? What are you talking about?"

"The story . . . Never mind, it just struck me as funny. . . ." Anyway, it didn't feel like a pea. More like a big bunch of turnips. It would be a lot to put up with for a whole week.

She heard Kat breathing softly in her sleep.

Lizabeth wished Kat was still awake. She felt lonely and far from home. She missed the soft glow of the outdoor gas lamp shining through her curtains. She missed her embroidered pillowcase. Every house has its very own nighttime creaks, she thought. The creaks at the cottage were unfamiliar. She longed to be at home, in her own bed.

She stared into the dark. She couldn't fall asleep. Why did everything seem so much worse at night? In the black silence she couldn't keep worrisome thoughts away.

Dear God, she prayed, bless Mother, Father, Chris, and Tracy, my friends and neighbors and all the ships at sea. That was her nightly prayer. Now she added: And please, God, keep Tracy safe tonight.

Lizabeth caught her breath and sat up straight in bed. The last time I was with Tracy, she thought, I screamed at her over some stupid ribbons!

"Lizabeth?" Kat murmured sleepily.

"I love Tracy."

"So do I." Kat reached up to take Lizabeth's hand. "She's my own little cousin. I prayed for her tonight."

"Thank you," Lizabeth said. "I did, too." God wouldn't

let anything hurt Tracy. Anyway, it wasn't something terrible like tuberculosis or cholera. . . .

"She'll get better soon."

"I know. Ada will know exactly what to do," Lizabeth said.

"Good night," Kat said. "Sleep tight."

"Good night."

Their hands stayed clasped together for a long time.

When Kat woke her the next morning, Lizabeth felt as though there were pebbles under her eyelids. She looked around the dim room.

"Isn't it awfully early?"

"Come on, sleepyhead," Kat said. "There are chores to do before school."

"*Chores* before school? What now?"

Kat's look told her she'd said the wrong thing again! Couldn't Kat appreciate that she was *trying*? It wasn't that easy to fit in with the Williamses' ways!

"For goodness' sake, Lizabeth. Don't you have to do *anything* at home?"

"We have Ada and the maids—though that new one seems lazy—and the laundress," Lizabeth said. "And I'm not going to feel guilty about it, either. I'm glad they're there. What good would it do anybody if I did their work and took their jobs away?"

"I guess that's true, but . . ." Kat looked thoughtful. "You should at least know what needs to be done. And who does it. So you'll respect their labor."

"You don't need to preach to me, Kat. I respect Ada. She just about raised us."

"It seems odd to call a grown-up woman by her first name," Kat said.

"Well, that's what we do." Lizabeth crossed her arms over her chest. "Anyway, I'll help out. So let's go do *chores*."

When they were dressed, Kat led her to the chicken coop behind the cottage. Before breakfast!

"It smells!" Lizabeth said before she could stop herself.

"Here, feed them while I collect the eggs."

"*Feed* them?" Chickens were pecking at Lizabeth's shoes and she backed away.

Kat laughed. "Pull yourself together, Lizabeth. All you need to do is scatter the seed!"

Lizabeth dropped some seed on the ground and that attracted more chickens to her feet. They were crowding around and clucking at her. They were aggressive!

Lizabeth took another step away and, oh, no! Her nice high-button black patent shoes were sinking into the disgusting *droppings*!

"Kat! Where are you? Get me out of this!"

The droppings were slippery and Lizabeth spread her arms to keep her balance. She couldn't fall into *that*! Her flapping arms made the chickens flutter away in all directions and feathers flew. Frantically, Lizabeth waved feathers away from her face.

"Stand still, you're scaring them!" Kat's voice came from somewhere behind her. Lizabeth whirled around and banged into Kat—and into the basket in Kat's hand. Broken eggs oozed all over the ground.

"Oh!" Lizabeth said. "Oh, I'm sorry." Yellow yolks dotted her black patent shoes.

Kat rolled her eyes. "Well, we won't have eggs for breakfast. Or anytime soon."

"I'm sorry. I meant to help."

Kat sighed. "I suppose you did."

It was all Lizabeth could do not to hang her head. "I'm sorry." Why, oh why, couldn't she do anything right at the Williamses'?

All the Williamses had breakfast together at the round table. Hotcakes. They were good. Actually,

Lizabeth preferred hotcakes to eggs. So maybe the morning wasn't such a disaster.

When Lizabeth was finished, she started for the door. She realized Kat wasn't following her and she turned back.

Everyone was busy: Jamie clearing the table, Kat washing dishes, Todd drying, Aunt Jean scrubbing the griddle, and Uncle Tom cleaning coals out of the stove. How very odd for Kat's father and brothers to be doing women's work. It had to be humiliating for them. Maybe that's what happened when people didn't have servants.

"Um . . . do you want me to do something?" Lizabeth asked.

There was a knock on the cottage door.

"I'll get it," Lizabeth said. Here was a chance to be helpful without getting her hands too dirty.

She opened the door and gasped in horror. Crazy Mary was on the threshold! The long gray hair blowing wildly in the wind made her even more grotesque. Close up, her bony face was a spiderweb of wrinkles. She extended a clawlike hand. Reaching for her!

In the nick of time Lizabeth slammed the door. She leaned against the closed door, her heart thumping. Thank goodness she'd reacted fast and kept a madwoman out! Maybe that would make up for everything else.

"Lizabeth? Who was it?" Aunt Jean asked.

"Crazy Mary! I just managed to . . ." Lizabeth was still catching her breath. She looked at the Williamses, expecting praise.

"You slammed the door on her? Why did you—" Aunt Jean went to open the door. She looked out and sighed. "Too late. She's running down the path."

"But it was Crazy Mary!" Lizabeth said.

"She comes by sometimes, and I wrap up some food for her," Aunt Jean said. "You shouldn't have turned her away like that."

"If she came here, she was hungry," Uncle Tom said. "I wish you'd asked us. She's just a sad old woman."

"I thought . . . I thought keeping her out was the right thing to do." No matter what Lizabeth did, she was getting everything wrong! It was embarrassing.

"She never comes in," Kat said. "She takes the food and runs away."

Now the Williamses thought she was uncharitable. But Crazy Mary was filthy and revolting! *And* crazy, which certainly could be dangerous. Maybe it was the Williamses who were wrong this time.

~seven~

odd and Jamie raced ahead of Lizabeth and Kat as they walked to school. From Lighthouse Lane, they turned into William McKinley Road. Strange, they were the only ones on the street. Lizabeth wondered why she didn't see the usual stream of children heading to school.

"We must be awfully late," Kat said.

What did Kat expect, with chicken coops and kitchen cleanup and Crazy Mary! It had been the *longest* morning.

Kat tugged at her. "Come on, let's run."

Ladies weren't supposed to dash helter-skelter down the street, Lizabeth thought, though that had never stopped Kat before. But Miss Cotter had all sorts of unpleasant punishments for lateness, like staying after school and washing the blackboard. So Lizabeth kept up with Kat. She held her long skirt out of the way, above her ankles. Actually, running was fun.

They stopped short on the front path to the school. "Uh-oh," Kat said.

Miss Cotter was standing at the entrance waiting for them. They had to be in big trouble!

"Sorry we're late, Miss Cotter," Kat gasped.

"Sorry, Miss Cotter," Lizabeth said. "We couldn't help it. We were attacked by some terrible chickens and—"

"I reached everyone who has a telephone," Miss Cotter said, "but since you don't have one at the lighthouse . . ." She looked harried. "I'm waiting for those I couldn't call. The mayor did promise that all of Cape Light would get telephone service soon. . . ."

Todd and Jamie were standing nearby with big grins on their faces. What was going on?

"School is closed, girls," Miss Cotter continued. "There's only a week left anyway, so it seems wisest."

"Why, Miss Cotter?" Kat asked. "What happened?"

"The scarlet fever," Miss Cotter said. "Mabel, the White twins, now Mark, and of course, your little cousin. Dr. Forbes said it's best not to have big groups gathering together."

"You mean school is over for the year?" Lizabeth asked.

Miss Cotter nodded. "I'm sorry. I feel dreadful

about the children who didn't have a chance to give their native culture reports. Maybe next term."

Amanda would be thrilled to forget about her Pygmies, Lizabeth thought.

"Lizabeth, I hope your sister gets well soon. Give my best to your parents. Oh, and if you see any of your classmates coming to school, please head them off."

"Yes, Miss Cotter."

"Thank you, Miss Cotter."

On the walk back to the lighthouse, Jamie was jumping up and down, chanting. "No more school, no more books! No more teacher's dirty looks!"

"Stop it!" Kat pinched his arm.

"But school is over!" Jamie protested.

"There's nothing to be happy about when people are sick," Kat said sternly.

"Oh." Jamie's face fell.

"Do you think there'll be an epidemic?" Todd asked.

"I think Miss Cotter is being cautious," Kat said, "so that we don't have one."

A chill swept through Lizabeth. Classmates were out all the time with colds and sore throats and no one thought anything of it. If they closed the school because of scarlet fever, it must be serious. Lizabeth didn't speak.

Her only thoughts were of Tracy.

They walked back toward the lighthouse and even Todd and Jamie were quiet.

They passed the bait-and-tackle shed on Lighthouse Lane. Mabel was out in front sweeping up. Kat and Lizabeth stopped to say hello, but they didn't get too close. Kat had a protective arm on Jamie's shoulder, holding him at a distance.

"It's all right," Mabel said with a big smile. "I'm over it. Dr. Forbes said I'm not contagious anymore."

Lizabeth looked her over carefully. Mabel seemed like her normal self. She was a little pale, but that could be from being indoors for such a long time.

"Was it awful?" Lizabeth asked.

"You know something? I don't even remember the whole week," Mabel said. "I was burning up and I stayed in bed and I felt terrible and then . . . I guess I slept a lot. It's funny not to remember all those days."

"I'm glad you're all better," Kat said.

"Oh, me, too! Now I can go out and play and go anywhere! And nobody in my family caught it, either."

Tracy, too, will get better soon, Lizabeth thought. Poor little Tracy, she must be burning up and feeling miserable now. But it'll be over soon.

She was so glad they'd run into Mabel! Now she could think about happier things. Like the Strawberry Festival. My goodness, May nineteenth was only nine days away! She'd better prepare to look her very best.

❦

Friday went by and then Saturday. Lizabeth really tried to get used to living at Kat's but it just wasn't relaxing.

Everyone was always rushing from one job to another, from lighthouse repairs to clean-up duties. The vegetable garden, the chickens, coal brought in and out, water brought in and out. The Williamses took care of their old horse themselves, though keeping him in a livery stable would be so much easier! Even little Jamie had chores. Who'd ever imagine there was so much to be done around one little cottage?

Lizabeth did mean to be helpful, but the Williamses seemed to have a set routine.

"No, thanks. I think I'd better do it," Kat said when Lizabeth halfheartedly volunteered to feed the chickens again.

❦

On Sunday they went to church. After the service, Rose told them that her father had seen Tracy. There was no change yet.

Everything quieted down for the Sabbath. On Monday, the chores started all over again.

It was already Monday, May fourteenth, Lizabeth thought. Tracy had been sick for seven days. That had to mean her scarlet fever would be gone soon. Of course, Tracy would get well. Of course, she would! The Strawberry Festival was in five days and Tracy would be there, a little pale maybe, but stuffing herself with strawberry shortcake.

At the cottage that afternoon, Aunt Jean asked, "Do you like chicken, Lizabeth? I thought I'd fry some up for dinner. And maybe corn fritters."

"That sounds delicious, Aunt Jean," Lizabeth said. She might have liked that if she could stop thinking of those dirty creatures that had pecked at her! But she was absolutely determined to be a considerate guest. "Delicious."

A hesitant expression must have crossed her face, though, because then Aunt Jean asked, "Lizabeth, tell me. Is there anything else you'd like?"

"Aunt Jean, if it's not too much trouble, I'd love to have a cucumber and a lemon."

Aunt Jean smiled. "That's fine. I'm going to the market now anyway."

When Aunt Jean returned, she handed over the produce in a mesh bag. Lizabeth thought, perfect, I'll have plenty of time. Kat was busy with *another* chore—something about weeding.

Lizabeth found the chopping block in the kitchen and sliced the cucumber. Then she squeezed the lemon into a small bowl. She took everything up to Kat's room.

She poured the lemon juice over her hair. She brushed it through and wrapped her hair in a towel. Lemon juice helped to keep it blond. Her hair used to be as light as Tracy's, but it had darkened over the years. By Strawberry Queen night, her hair would be golden and shimmering. Lemon juice would be more effective in sunlight, but that would mean taking a terrible chance of darkening her complexion or even getting freckles! That was why she carried a parasol everywhere.

Lizabeth sighed contentedly and lay down on the bed. She closed her eyes and covered them with cucumber slices. If she did this every day between now and the Strawberry Festival, there wouldn't be the slightest hint of puffiness. The cool cucumber felt so good. In spite of the lumpy mattress, Lizabeth dozed off.

The door creaked open. "Dinner will be ready soon and if you're going to fix the salad—" Kat's voice.

Lizabeth sat up, startled. "Salad?"

"Lizabeth! *What* are you doing with that cucumber?"

Lizabeth removed the slices and blinked. "It's a beauty secret, Kat. To make your eyes—"

"I don't believe this. Ma was so pleased that you wanted to help out and make a salad. I thought I'd find you in the kitchen."

"*What* salad?"

"Cucumber-and-lemon salad! Everyone assumed . . . What did you do with the lemon?"

"It's in my hair. For blondness and shine."

Kat rolled her eyes.

"What's the matter now?" Lizabeth asked.

"That's *food*, Lizabeth. We don't use food for beauty secrets!" Kat shook her head and began to laugh. "Sometimes I think you're from another universe. What are we going to tell Ma?"

"I have to beat the competition for Strawberry Queen, don't I?" Lizabeth said. "I found a wonderful book at the Pelican. *Beauty Secrets of the Ages.* Everyone knows about biting your lips and pinching your cheeks to make them rosy. I have to do *extra.*"

"I think you've done enough extra!"

"Is there any nightshade growing around Durham Point?" Lizabeth asked.

"Deadly nightshade? No! I sure hope not," Kat said.

"I read that if you put some in your eyes, it dilates the pupils and makes them look ever so large and shiny."

"Nightshade is poison!" Kat said.

"I guess you're supposed to use just the tiniest bit. Do you know the other name for nightshade? Belladonna. It means beautiful lady in Italian. That proves that it beautified a lot of ladies." Lizabeth frowned. "I don't know if you're supposed to use the berries or the leaves. The book didn't say."

"I think there's some poison ivy in the back that we couldn't get rid of," Kat said. "Do you have a beauty secret for that?"

"Don't be silly!" Sometimes Kat was so immature!

"Lizabeth, this isn't funny anymore. Nightshade is really poisonous."

"I wouldn't *eat* it. I'm talking about just a bit in my eyes."

"I think you'd better stop reading that book." Kat looked closely at Lizabeth. "You wouldn't really use something dangerous, would you?"

"I don't know. You're kind of scaring me." Lizabeth

shrugged. "I don't know *exactly* how to apply night-shade. But if I did, just for that *one* evening, for the Strawberry Festival. . . ."

"Being Strawberry Queen can't be that important to you," Kat said.

"Anybody would want to be Strawberry Queen."

"All right, it would be fun. I'm not saying anything against it—and I'd love to see you win—but you care so much, you're talking about poisoning yourself!"

"It's not only for Strawberry Queen," Lizabeth said, "though that's my dream, of course. It's about being as pretty as I possibly can. So someone will fall madly in love with me."

"There are lots of other reasons for someone to love you."

"Prettiness is what counts, and if you think it doesn't, that's plain childish."

Kat looked thoughtful. "It's nice to feel pretty, but I wouldn't for a minute want someone to love me for that. I'd want someone to love me for . . . well, my talent. And because I'm maybe funny, or adventurous, or brave sometimes. And mostly kindhearted."

"You *are* all those things, Kat."

"I mean, I'd expect more from someone who's supposed to love me. More than, 'Oh, good, she has nice shiny eyes.'"

That's easy for Kat to say, Lizabeth thought, because she does have a special talent. And people are always drawn to her.

❧

When Uncle Tom came in for dinner that night, he planted a kiss on Kat's nose. "The best freckle, second from the right," he said. "How's my favorite daughter?"

"I'm your *only* daughter!"

"If I had ten more, you'd still be my favorite!"

The very same routine had been repeated every night since Lizabeth had been at Kat's. Kat ducked her head when she noticed Lizabeth listening, probably feeling a little childish. But she has to be pleased, too, Lizabeth thought. Father would never be that affectionate with me or Tracy.

No one loves me that much. It's a good thing I have big blue eyes, Lizabeth thought, and a wardrobe full of exquisite clothes. She pictured the Strawberry Queen dress hanging in her closet at home. Heavens, the Festival was just around the corner! Tracy might take longer than Mabel to get well. She'd better get that dress and have it ready at Kat's.

At dinner Lizabeth dutifully nibbled at the fried chicken and corn fritters. She was grateful that no one said anything about another course. Except for Jamie, who piped up with, "When do we get the cucumber salad?" But Aunt Jean shushed him right away. And Uncle Tom's lips twitched only a little, holding back his laughter. Kat must have warned her parents. So Lizabeth wasn't *too* embarrassed and could keep her mind on making a plan. She'd just have to sneak into her room at home when everyone was asleep and grab the dress.

Tonight she'd climb up the rose trellis that led to the window of her room. Chris had used the side trellis more than once to sneak out. If it could hold him, it was certainly strong enough for her. But what if the Williamses caught her leaving the cottage? Or if her parents heard her? She'd be sent away to Pittsfield for sure! But she couldn't do without that dress. She'd have to take the chance.

ᴇ*eight*ᴇ

It seemed to Lizabeth that the evening was stretching on and on. She sat with Kat during her lighthouse shift and worried about all the things that could go wrong. Uncle Tom would be in the lighthouse tower for the overnight shift. The most difficult moment would be leaving the cottage and getting onto the road unseen.

"You're so fidgety tonight," Kat said. "What's the matter?"

"Nothing," Lizabeth answered. She glanced at her cousin. Should she ask Kat for help? It would be so much easier with Kat for company. It might even be fun. After all, Kat was the adventurous one. She even stowed away on a fishing boat last year to go to Boston!

"Kat, I'm going to . . ." Lizabeth started. Then she bit her lip. Better not. Kat didn't understand how very important the right dress was. She'd just say to wear something else. She'd talk her out of it.

"You're going to what?" Kat asked.

"Nothing," Lizabeth mumbled.

Finally the shift was over. Finally they got ready for bed. Kat burrowed into her bedroll. Lizabeth listened to the sound of her cousin's breathing.

"Kat?" Lizabeth whispered.

No answer. Kat was definitely asleep.

Lizabeth got out of bed, pulled off her nightgown, and dressed in the dark. She groped for her shoes on the floor and almost bumped into Sunshine! She had forgotten all about the dog lying at Kat's side. He raised his head. Please, don't bark! "Good dog," she whispered.

She stopped, held her breath, and waited. Kat continued to breathe evenly. Sunshine gazed at her but remained quietly at Kat's side.

Lizabeth tiptoed out of the room and into the hall. Todd and Jamie had gone to bed earlier. There was no sound from their room.

The downstairs of the cottage was dark. Aunt Jean had to be asleep, too. She always went to sleep right after kitchen cleanup because she had to get up for the dawn lighthouse shift. Lizabeth counted on them all being too exhausted to wake up, what with all their endless chores. She slipped out the front door.

There was enough moonlight to see by. Lizabeth stayed close to the bushes along the front path, hoping to blend into the shadows. If she was lucky, Uncle Tom's attention would be on the ocean now.

Lizabeth reached Lighthouse Lane. No commotion from the lighthouse. No one calling out her name.

She walked fast along Lighthouse Lane. At first, she was exhilarated that she'd made it. But then—it was so dark. Rustling sounds in the underbrush seemed to be following her. It had to be a rabbit. Or a squirrel. But what if there were stray dogs? Mean, hungry ones . . . She ran. She ran past the docks, past the boatyard, past the tackle-and-bait shed. Not one light was on. Not one person was out on the lane.

She ran until she was out of breath. She went back to walking fast. The road she'd known all her life was eerie in the moonlight. She tried to focus on the peaceful sound of the ocean lapping against the shore. But anything could be hiding in the shadows.

Please, God, I just want to go home.

She was relieved when she reached the paved section of Lighthouse Lane. Here were the nicest houses, houses more like hers.

Soon she stood on the path to her home. How

beautiful it looked. How she'd missed it! The gas lamps in front were off. The house was dark.

Lizabeth hesitated in front of the trellis. Her window looked so high up. She wasn't used to climbing. That simply wasn't a skill a lady would ever need! But this was an emergency.

She put her foot on the first rung and then the next. It was hard. The rose branches were getting in her way. Another rung and another.

The trellis creaked. Lizabeth stopped short. It might be breaking! And what if Mother and Father heard?

Shakily she climbed on. Thorns tore at her, her skirt tangled around her feet. She tottered unbalanced. Don't look down, she told herself.

Her window was just above. Oh, what if it was locked! She'd never thought of that. If I've gone through all of this to get my dress, Lizabeth thought, then I deserve to be Strawberry Queen. I've earned it.

The window slid open easily. That had to be a good sign. She was afraid to let her foot leave the trellis. She didn't move for a long, uncertain moment before she dared reach for the sill. Then she was up and over. She landed with a bounce on her bed. She had almost forgotten how deliciously soft it was.

It was easy enough to find the strawberry dress hanging separately from the others in the closet. She put it gently over her arm. She'd never manage to climb down with it! Another thing she hadn't planned.

Lizabeth tiptoed to the door of her room and opened it. She could hear Father snoring at the other end of the house. All right. She'd take a chance on creeping down the stairs and out the back door.

A night-light shone through the open doorway of Tracy's room. How could she possibly leave without seeing her?

She expected to find Tracy looking angelic in her sleep. But Tracy was thrashing in her bed, tangled in her sheets and whimpering. Tracy was suffering!

Lizabeth felt something squeeze her heart. "Tracy?" she whispered. "Are you awake?"

"Water," Tracy murmured.

Lizabeth sat down on the bed. In the dim light her little sister's eyes looked sunken deep into their sockets.

"Lizabeth?"

"I'm here," Lizabeth whispered. She poured water into a glass from the carafe on the nightstand.

Tracy was too weak to sit up. Lizabeth put her arm around her and propped her up while she took a few sips. She was shocked by the heat coming off the small body.

"Oh, Trace!"

Tracy pushed the glass away and sank back into the pillow. "I'm hot," she whimpered.

There was a folded washcloth on the nightstand. It looked like it had been used for cold compresses. Lizabeth dipped an end in water and gently wiped Tracy's flushed face. It was drawn and very small.

"Is that better?" Lizabeth asked.

"I'm sorry, Lizabeth," Tracy whispered.

"You'll get well soon. I know you will." Lizabeth stroked her hair. It was damp and sticky with sweat. "I'm so sorry you're sick."

"It's punish . . . punishment," Tracy said. "God is mad at me."

Lizabeth's spine tingled in fear. Had Tracy become delirious?

"I'm sorry," Tracy whispered.

"No, Tracy, God isn't mad at you. I promise."

"Your pink velvet ribbon. I took it. 'Cause it was so pretty. And . . . and I lied."

"Oh, cupcake, I don't care about the ribbon. I'm so sorry I yelled at you. I didn't mean it."

"I'm sick 'cause I was bad." Tracy moaned. "Lizabeth, I'm hot."

"No, no, you're a good girl." Tears filled Lizabeth's eyes. "You're sick because . . ." She didn't know what to give for a reason. It wasn't fair! "Because . . . because the sickness was in Cape Light and you caught it. Lots of people did. You know Mabel, don't you? She had the sickness and she's all well now."

"Mabel, the big girl? Was she bad, too?"

"No, Tracy. No one was bad. You were *never* bad." Lizabeth held back a sob and dampened the towel again. "Please don't think that." She wiped Tracy's face and neck. "I love you. We all love you. Mother and Father, Chris, Ada, Kat—"

"I'm scared to go to sleep," Tracy whispered.

"Don't be scared. God loves you. Do you want to pray with me?"

Tracy nodded.

"Dear God, please help Tracy get well soon. Tracy and I ask that she has good dreams tonight, sweet dreams about pussycats and baby dolls and spring flowers. Please let her sleep tight in your loving arms and wake up bright-eyed in the morning. Amen."

Lizabeth was surprised by the sense of peace that

came over her. She was the least religious of all her friends. Tracy's face, too, looked peaceful now.

"You forgot God bless Mother, Father, Chris, our friends and neighbors . . ." Tracy's eyes were barely open. ". . . and all the ships at sea."

"You're right." Lizabeth's voice broke. "God bless us all."

Tracy snuggled against the pillow clutching her teddy bear.

Lizabeth straightened the sheet. "Do you think you can sleep now?"

"Uh-huh," Tracy murmured faintly. Soon her eyelids were closed, lashes curving against her cheeks. She was breathing softly through partly open lips. It hurt Lizabeth to see how the fever had cracked and parched the lips that had been like rosebuds.

"I have to leave before anyone sees me," Lizabeth whispered. She kissed the sleeping child's brow. "I promise I'll be back."

🌿

Lizabeth walked back to Kat's cottage along Lighthouse Lane carrying the dress over her arm. This time she wasn't aware of the night noises and deep shadows. She was blinded by tears. It was her fault that Tracy was tormented by that stupid ribbon. She had been a terrible big sister.

Dear God, Lizabeth whispered, please help me do better. When she gets well, I'll play with Tracy more. I'll pay more attention. She carries *Sleeping Beauty* and *The Ugly Duckling* around, looking for someone to read to her. A sob caught in Lizabeth's throat. Please, God, let me have that chance.

On the path to Kat's cottage, Lizabeth stopped to pull herself together. She wiped her face with her sleeve and took a deep breath.

Then through the front door, up the stairs, and into Kat's room. She dropped the strawberry dress over a chair.

Sunshine raised his head and gave a questioning yip.

"Shhh, good dog," Lizabeth whispered.

Kat stirred in her bedroll. "What time is it?"

"It's still night," Lizabeth said. "Go back to sleep."

"Wait—why are you dressed?" Kat asked. "What's going on?"

"I saw Tracy."

Kat sat up. "Tracy?"

"She doesn't look good, Kat. She . . ." There was a lump in Lizabeth's throat.

"How did you see Tracy? Were you with her?"

"I went home." Lizabeth's voice was scratchy with fatigue. She pulled on her nightgown. "I had to get the strawberry dress and I went into Tracy's room. She—"

Kat bolted out of the bedroll and faced Lizabeth, her eyes blazing. "How could you? How could you break quarantine for a *dress*? You exposed yourself to *scarlet fever*!"

"Well, that's my business, isn't it?"

"It's my business, too! You don't care about anyone but yourself."

Lizabeth was stunned. "I don't *care*?" she repeated. She was devastated by Tracy's suffering. She had expected comfort from Kat.

"I know you're self-centered and vain, but this is too much. Even for you. How dare you put Todd and Jamie and my whole family in danger!"

"Oh. I never thought of that."

"What do you think quarantine is for?" Kat glared at her, hands on her hips. "Is there anything in your head besides beauty contests and—and nightshade?"

Lizabeth's eyes widened with hurt.

"If you've brought the fever here to my little brothers . . ." Kat sputtered in anger. "For nothing more than—than *this*!" She fingered a fold of the dress and flung it aside.

"You're so mean. Rough and mean!" Lizabeth lashed out in her pain. "And . . . and heartless! You stomp on other people's feelings. Everything has to be your way. I'm tired of you rolling your eyes at me and directing me. Ever since I've been here—"

"If you don't like it—" Kat started.

"I'll leave," Lizabeth finished. "You're right, I don't like it here. I don't like *you*!"

They stared at each other. The few feet between them felt like miles.

Lizabeth lowered her eyes first. It was true she hadn't even considered that she might infect Kat and her family.

She wouldn't cry in front of Kat. She wouldn't! She pulled her suitcase out from under the bed.

"It's the middle of the night," Kat said. "You have no place to go."

"I don't care."

"I suppose we can hope you didn't catch the fever." Kat's voice softened a little. "How is Tracy?"

"I started to tell you and you didn't even bother to listen," Lizabeth said bitterly.

"If you weren't with her for very long, you probably didn't . . . Look, I won't say anything to Ma and get her all upset if I don't have to. Just keep a distance from my brothers. And you'd better wash your dishes separately and wash them *well*. Boil the water and—"

"I can figure that out for myself," Lizabeth said.

"And if you start to feel even a little bit sick, you've got to tell right away."

Lizabeth opened her suitcase halfheartedly. "It's easiest if I leave."

"Go to bed, Lizabeth." Kat blew out an exasperated breath. "For goodness' sake, just go to bed."

Lizabeth lay down and stared into the darkness. She knew that Kat wasn't sleeping either. The silence between them felt heavy. There was nothing left to say.

~nine~

The next morning Amanda and Rose came over to the lighthouse tower.

"You should see what's going on in town," Amanda said. "People are walking around with masks on. It's spooky."

"Everyone's scared," Rose said.

"You never know how people are going to act," Amanda said. "Some only want to keep to themselves, taking no chances. You can't blame them."

"Father says it makes sense for people to be afraid of being contaminated," Rose said, "but Cape Light people have been wonderful about caring for terribly sick neighbors who are alone."

"My father saw Mrs. Cornell at the Whites'," Amanda said, "helping out with the twins without a thought for herself."

"There are so many people who are ill, Lizabeth,"

Rose said. "The Whites, both Mr. *and* Mrs., two of the Halloran children . . . the rest have been sent out of town."

"All three Brewster children," Amanda added. "Mrs. Brewster comes to church every day to pray for them."

"It seems to hit young children the most," Rose said.

"Has your father seen Tracy again?" Lizabeth asked.

Rose nodded. "He sees her every day on his rounds."

"What does he say?"

"Honestly, he doesn't say much of anything. He comes home very late and dead tired. They're just waiting for Tracy's fever to break."

"But isn't there something to do? Besides *waiting*?" Lizabeth asked. "It's been a week already."

Amanda squeezed her hand. "Tracy will be fine, I just know it."

"There's no medicine for it," Rose said. "The only thing is cold compresses to cool her. And something nourishing if she can keep it down."

"Ada makes the most wonderful beef broth. Tracy loves it," Lizabeth said.

"Didn't you know? Ada's not at your house,

Lizabeth," Rose said. "She's been at her sister Leda's. Leda's too sick to take care of her own children."

Ada not there? Tracy would miss her!

"Don't worry," Rose said softly. "Almost everyone gets well."

"When it's all over it'll be like a bad dream," Amanda said. "You'll see."

Lizabeth gazed out of the windows. How could it be such a perfect spring day when she felt so troubled? Fluffy white clouds drifted lazily across a blue sky. The sea was calm today and a beautiful blue-gray.

"It seems strange that school ended so suddenly," Amanda said.

"Well, it makes sense," Kat said. She had been unusually quiet all morning. "No one should be put at risk for no good reason." She gave Lizabeth a cutting look.

Lizabeth turned away and caught Amanda's puzzled glance.

"Lizabeth," Rose said. "Did you hear the Strawberry Festival has been cancelled? No crowds, no large gatherings. The Strawberry Queen event too."

"It doesn't matter," Lizabeth said dully.

"There's always next year," Amanda said. "You can enter next year."

"I'm sorry. I know you were looking forward to it," Rose said.

"I don't care," Lizabeth said, and realized that she honestly didn't anymore. Not from the moment she had seen Tracy.

"You don't?" Kat's voice was sharp. "As of last night, it was the most important thing in the world! More important than *anyone*!"

Lizabeth matched her tone. "I said I *don't care*! Is that so hard to understand?"

Amanda looked from one to the other. "What's going on with the two of you?"

Lizabeth hoped Kat wouldn't explain. There wasn't much she could say in her own defense. Amanda and Rose would surely side with Kat.

Lizabeth had never thought much about it before, but Amanda had been Kat's friend first. Kat's family practically adopted her in those terrible months after her mother died. Lizabeth hadn't exactly *avoided* her, but Amanda's grief had made Lizabeth feel too uncomfortable. Well, she'd only been seven then.

And Rose and Kat became especially close when Kat helped her care for her horse. Lizabeth had gone to Clayton Stables a few times, but she'd really done . . .

nothing. Except pose in her scarlet riding jacket, she remembered now with embarrassment.

"What is it?" Rose asked. "What happened?"

"We had a disagreement," Kat said stiffly.

"I don't want to talk about it," Lizabeth muttered.

"Well, if it was just a little disagreement . . ." Rose started.

"It wasn't *little*. Things were said that can't be unsaid," Kat told them. "It's too late."

Amanda looked distressed. "Come on, you've been best friends since . . . since you were born!"

"We were forced on each other," Kat said. "By our mothers."

"We're cousins, not friends," Lizabeth said. "We have nothing in common."

"Don't do this, please," Amanda pleaded.

"Nothing could be that serious," Rose added.

"It's supposed to be the four of us together, remember?" Amanda said.

"Four best friends, forever," Rose said. "Don't spoil it!"

"I don't care what happened. You've got to apologize to each other right now." Amanda was almost in tears. "You've got to!"

Kat looked out the window. Lizabeth studied her feet.

"When I came to Cape Light," Rose said, "I thought the three of you had the best friendship I'd ever seen. I was so happy to be included. You can't stay mad. Not here, not in our special place."

Kat and Lizabeth exchanged guarded looks.

"Kat," Amanda said. "Lizabeth. Please!"

After a long pause, Kat spoke. "I don't think I was wrong but I guess I'm sorry about some of the things I said. Though not all."

"I'm not saying you're wrong—you're not—but I did what I had to do. You could have tried to understand. I couldn't be there and not see . . ." Lizabeth took a breath. "I guess I'm sorry for what I said, too. I suppose I do like you. Some of the time, anyway."

"I worry about Tracy, too," Kat said softly. "I do understand."

"You were mean," Lizabeth said. "You have a terrible temper."

"Well, so do you. And I'm *not* heartless!" Kat paused. "Lizabeth, I want you to know—I wasn't upset only because of my brothers. I was mad at you for risking *yourself*."

Amanda and Rose looked at each other in confusion.

"All right, good enough," Rose said.

Amanda took the other three girls' hands and clasped them together. "Four of us, together," she said.

"Four, together," Rose repeated and Kat and Lizabeth joined in.

"Forever!" they finished. Lizabeth felt so comforted by the warmth of their friendship. Even if she hadn't quite earned it.

۵

When the Williamses finished lunch Lizabeth jumped up from the table first. She went to the well outside and brought back the heavy bucket of water. She heated water on the stove and prepared to wash the dishes.

"It's supposed to be my turn," Todd said uneasily.

"I'll do them," Lizabeth said. "I want to help out."

Todd grinned. "If you *want* to, that sure is all right with me!" He zoomed out of the kitchen.

The soap was harsh on Lizabeth's hands. No wonder. Aunt Jean made it herself out of lye and grease! Once she was home and back to normal, she'd *slather* her hands with her milk-and-almond lotion.

Later in the afternoon when Aunt Jean finished washing the laundry in the sink, Lizabeth volunteered to do the wringing.

Aunt Jean looked surprised. "It's hard work, Lizabeth."

"I can do it." It *was* hard. Turning the hand wringer made her arms ache. But somehow straining her muscles eased her mind.

"Thank you," Aunt Jean said. "Then maybe I'll take a little nap before I start dinner."

Lizabeth shrugged apologetically. "I don't know how to cook."

"No one expects you to," Kat said.

When Lizabeth finished wringing the clothes, her arms were limp. She helped Kat hang the wash on the line outside. I've never had a clothespin in my hands in my entire life, she thought. Not that I was missing much!

She pinned one corner of a white sheet while Kat pinned another.

"You don't have to prove anything to me," Kat said.

"I'm not trying to," Lizabeth answered. She wasn't sure, but maybe she was proving something to herself. It felt surprisingly good to be useful. "Staying busy keeps me from thinking too much."

Kat nodded. "I know how that is."

Lizabeth was glad she and Kat were friends again. She was sorry that she was going to spoil that soon. She had to go to Tracy, no matter what Kat thought. She had to see with her own eyes if Tracy's fever was breaking.

~ten~

Lizabeth kept Kat company in the lighthouse tower during her evening shift. She watched the light revolve through the rapidly darkening night. She was too anxious to sit still. She couldn't wait for hours until everyone was asleep.

"Kat, I'm going down, all right?"

Kat nodded. "You must be all tired out."

"No, just feeling restless," Lizabeth said. "Maybe I'll take a walk." She couldn't quite face Kat.

"All right. See you in the room later."

"See you."

This time she didn't have to worry about anyone spotting her on the path to Lighthouse Lane. Sunshine followed her a little way and then he turned back toward the cottage.

Lizabeth continued on the road. Past Wharf Way and the docks, past the abandoned fishermen's huts that were meant to be torn down long ago, past the bait-and-tackle shop, past Alveira's Boatyard, up the hill, and onto the paved section of Lighthouse Lane.

She hid in the shadows when she heard the clop-clop of a horse. In the moonlight, she could just make out Dr. Forbes guiding his horse and carriage up the path to his house. Otherwise the lane was deserted. He must be coming back from visiting patients, she thought. So late in the night! She didn't know him well—only as "Rose's father"—but she was filled with respect for him.

When Lizabeth was sure he was inside, she continued to her house.

The light was on in the downstairs parlor. Were her parents there? Would they hear her? She knew it was wrong to break quarantine again, but she didn't care. *Nothing* could keep her from going to Tracy!

Lizabeth climbed up the trellis, wincing at each creak. A thorn tore at her dress. The rip was horribly loud in the stillness. She stopped at the top to peer through her window. Through the open door of her room she could catch a glimpse of the hallway in the faint beam from Tracy's night-light. Mother and Father! They were in silhouette in Tracy's doorway. Lizabeth was overcome with longing to rush into Mother's arms. She watched them leave Tracy's room and head toward the top of the staircase.

Whew! It was a good thing she had stopped to look first! If they caught her, they'd surely ship her off to Pittsfield. She could imagine Father roaring at her, something about "out of harm's way."

Lizabeth couldn't see the stairs from the trellis. She gave them time to get downstairs. *If* they were going downstairs. She couldn't teeter on top of the trellis forever. She had to take a chance.

The window of her room was still open and she slipped in. She removed her shoes and tiptoed across the floor slowly, carefully. She was afraid to breathe. She couldn't make a sound. All clear in the hallway. She crept into Tracy's room.

Lizabeth tiptoed to her bed. Tracy's eyes were wide open.

"It's me," Lizabeth whispered. "I promised I'd come back to see you."

There was no reaction from Tracy.

"It's me, Lizabeth." She put her hand on her little sister's forehead. Burning! How she had hoped and prayed to find Tracy better tonight!

"Tracy?" she whispered.

Tracy stared directly at Lizabeth, but her eyes were unfocused. As if she's looking *through* me, Lizabeth thought and she felt her stomach clutch.

"Tracy?"

Tracy moved her head back and forth, agitated. "I don't *want* to leave the party!" Her faint voice was raspy. "Not yet!"

Lizabeth touched Tracy's shoulder and Tracy pulled away.

"More ice cream," Tracy said, with that terrible raspy voice. "I want to stay!"

Her words made Lizabeth shudder. "Tracy, it's all right," she whispered. "Of course you'll stay here with us."

"Leave me alone! Don't make me go!"

Prickles chilled the back of Lizabeth's neck. It's as if Tracy isn't *here*, she thought. Is this what *delirious* means? Is it normal for this to happen just before the fever breaks?

Lizabeth reached for Tracy again and stopped her hand in midair. Tracy's eyes had closed. She seemed to have fallen asleep. She was taking deep, wheezing breaths through her open mouth.

Lizabeth softly kissed Tracy's cheek. Burning!

She watched and waited helplessly. The only sound

in her ears was the wheezing. But then—Father's voice. She could hear his distress though she couldn't make out the words. And Mother's weeping. The click of Mother's shoes at the bottom of the stairs! Quick, before Mother comes around the curve of the staircase!

Lizabeth moved through the shadows of the hall and slipped into her own room. She heard Mother's voice at Tracy's bedside and then Father's. All their attention would be on Tracy. She could make it down the trellis. . . .

Lizabeth jumped from the bottom rung and crept alongside the azaleas on the front path. She was numb with shock. She walked a block on Lighthouse Lane before she realized that she'd left her shoes behind.

She walked another block before she suddenly stopped and thought, Where am I going? I can't go back to Kat's again. I've been exposed to scarlet fever *twice*. I can't bring it to Amanda's or Rose's house. Or anyone's. Lizabeth bit her lip. I have no place to go.

∽eleven∽

L izabeth wandered to the village green. It was strange to feel the grass between her toes.

She cut across the square of lawn. She came to the statue of the lost fisherman in the center. Under the three-quarter moon, deep shadows accented the folds of his stone slicker and the cross-hatched fishing net over his shoulder. In the hazy light, he seemed about to get off his pedestal and walk over to South Street.

Lizabeth remembered when the *North Star* sank six years ago. Eight men went down with her. At first there was going to be a memorial plaque engraved with the names of all the Cape Light men lost at sea over the years. Then the town council realized that more names would have to be continually added. Donations were collected to put up the statue instead, to honor all of them, past and future. Cape Light was so pleasant and peaceful, but it was a seafaring town that depended on an often treacherous sea.

Death had never touched anyone close to her, Lizabeth realized, except for Amanda. She shivered. She wouldn't think about death. She wouldn't! Maybe Tracy hadn't been delirious at all. If she had just awakened from a deep sleep, it made sense that she was still halfway in a dream. What was the harm in a dream about a party? Someday she and Tracy would laugh about it.

Lizabeth sat down on the bench in front of the courthouse and brushed grass and pebbles from her soles. In daylight the bench was the property of the old men who gathered there to argue, divided for and against whatever President Teddy Roosevelt was doing next. They'd pass hours there, munching doughnuts from the bakery. . . .

The bakery was shuttered now. The busy general store/post office was nothing but a dark looming shape. Moonlight glimmered on the red-and-white pole in front of the barbershop. Cape Light looked deserted. She had never felt so all alone.

What was she going to do? She had never thought beyond seeing Tracy. Where could she go now? Maybe spend the night right here on the bench. It was as good a plan as any. She'd think more clearly in the morning.

Lizabeth twisted into a comfortable position on the

wooden planks and used her arm for a pillow.

Dear God, Lizabeth whispered, please keep Tracy safe tonight. She's still so small and innocent. She wakes up happy every morning, full of wonder for the new day. She doesn't know that anything bad could happen. Please God, take care of my little sister.

Far away a dog barked. It would be an endless, lonely night. She heard a new sound: the whistles of gusts of wind.

Lizabeth sat up. Clouds covered the moon. Now she could barely see more than a foot ahead. New leaves of the big maples around the square rustled. Lizabeth hugged her arms around her chest. The temperature was dropping. The air felt heavy and damp.

It can't rain, she thought. Please, not tonight! She had to find shelter. But where? She couldn't think. Somewhere. . . .

The Mill Pond! There was a little shed on the far side, where they'd put on their skates or stash hot cocoa when the pond froze over in the winter.

Lizabeth had to go slowly in the dark, feeling her way on the road. The distance to the pond had never seemed longer. Ow! Something cut deep into her heel. A sharp stone. She dug it out, but now she was limping.

She kept her mind on the shed and forced herself forward. Another painful step, a little further . . .

Lizabeth heard water lapping against the shore. The Mill Pond! A flood of memories washed over her. Tracy, learning to skate last winter. It was Chris who patiently held her hand, though all his friends were zooming around the ice. Chris did have a tender side, Lizabeth realized. One that he saved mostly for Tracy.

The last time they went, Tracy was skating on her own with a huge, proud grin. Lizabeth could almost see it: Tracy falling, her little face crumpling but refusing to cry, picking herself up and starting off again. Lizabeth's heart turned over. Nothing ever stopped that brave little girl.

Lizabeth was making her way around the pond when the drizzle began. Last week she would have said a drizzle was good for her dewy complexion. Had her mind really been on nothing else?

She had reached the shed when the rain became heavier. Thank goodness she'd made it just in time! She felt her way around the wooden sides. Here was the door! It was latched shut with a heavy iron lock. Lizabeth was stunned with disbelief. She rattled and rattled the chain. No use. She pounded desperately at the door. She pounded until her fists were sore.

She stood in misery as the rain drenched her. Her dress was plastered to her body. Her soaked petticoat weighed her down. Water ran from her hair down her face, down her neck, along her arms. If she didn't get out of the rain, she'd surely get sick—if she wasn't already.

She heard the first rumblings of thunder in the distance. She had to do something! But what? *What?* Kat's cottage, Rose's, Amanda's—so warm and cozy, forbidden to her now when she needed her friends the most.

Her dripping hair ribbon was blown in front of her face. She pulled it off. She was breathing with rapid, panicked gasps. Stop it, she told herself. *Think!*

The abandoned fishermen's huts! There were three of them down near the docks. Ice fishermen had used them before they became too dilapidated. But they were still partially standing, they still had roofs, she thought. All that long way to the docks—but somewhere to go.

Lizabeth retraced her steps back to Lighthouse Lane. She lost track of how long she'd been walking. She could hardly see in the pelting rain. Then the first bolts of lightning scared her. Stay away from trees, Lizabeth remembered. They're hit first in a thunderstorm. But the lane was lined with trees! There was nothing she could do except keep going.

She limped, favoring her right foot. In the dark, she veered off the road. When she brushed against the bushes, she redirected her steps back to the path. She went from paving to dirt road, her feet squishing in mud. She gave in to the streams of water running down her body. When lightning came, she learned to use the moment of visibility to check her direction.

She walked and walked, and suddenly she thought, Maybe this is my walkabout. She had nothing: no shoes, no clothing but a torn and sopping dress, none of the trimmings that had been so important to her. I'm stripped bare, Lizabeth thought. It's just me now, down to the basics. Is this where I meet myself?

Who would she meet? A girl whose entire soul had been wrapped up in becoming a beauty queen, with *Beauty Secrets of the Ages* as her bible? A girl who thought her pretty dresses made her special? So very smug and so dependent on being rich—is *that* all I am? Her tears mixed with the rain running down her cheeks. Not anymore, please, God—I can be better than that!

Lizabeth was tempted to sink helplessly to the ground. No! She wiped her eyes. No, I'll go on walking and I *will* reach the huts. And I will *not* seek help where I might infect someone else.

In a flash of lightning, Lizabeth spotted the first tumbledown hut. She almost cried with gratitude as she rushed toward it. The door was half off its hinges. It was easy to get in. She bumped her knee on something—a crate? She went deep into the shed until she hit the far wall. It was dry back here. Blessedly dry!

Lizabeth went limp with relief. A haven at last. She sank down to the rough, splintery floor and huddled into a ball to keep warm. I'll make it through the night, she thought, and there'll be another morning and God's warm, comforting sun.

Suddenly she heard the door's hinges creak. The wind? No, the door was being *pushed* open. Someone was coming inside! Lizabeth gasped and scrambled to her feet.

"Who's there?" a hoarse voice called.

Lizabeth was too uneasy to answer. She shrank against the wall. She heard the scratch of a match. She saw the flare of a candle being lit. Above its wavering flickers was a grotesque bony face.

Crazy Mary!

twelve

"Who's there?" Crazy Mary's hoarse voice repeated. "Answer me!"

Lizabeth cowered against the far wall. Her heart was racing.

"Don't think I can't hear you! Show yourself!" Crazy Mary lit another candle. Now there were two, placed in hurricane lamps on a crate. Their light wavered unsteadily throughout the hut. "This is *my* place!"

"I'll . . . I'll go." Lizabeth was trembling.

Crazy Mary, covered by a dripping tarpaulin, was blocking the doorway. Did she dare run past her? She was afraid to get close.

"Please. If you move from the door, I'll go. Let me . . . let me go."

Crazy Mary took a step toward her.

"Don't come near me! I might have scarlet fever," Lizabeth threatened.

"What do I care about the fever?" Crazy Mary chortled, and her laughter was horribly out of place.

"Let me out," Lizabeth begged.

"Foolish girl! You'll catch your death in the rain." Crazy Mary peered at her. "You're a young one, are you? Tell me how old."

"Thir—thirteen," Lizabeth stammered. She saw a neat pile of rags against the wall and a dented tin dish. There was a big straw bag stuffed with pieces of clothing and what seemed to be a faded family Bible. She had stumbled into the hut that served as Crazy Mary's home! "I didn't mean any harm, I—" If she could somehow edge around her . . .

"Are you a friend of my Kevin?" Crazy Mary asked.

Who was Kevin? What was she supposed to say?

"No, no, I get mixed up." Crazy Mary groaned. "It was six years ago Kevin was fifteen. Nineteen hundred, turn of the century. Six years."

Crazy Mary was an old woman, that's all, Lizabeth told herself. She couldn't be very strong. Lizabeth gathered her courage. I can force my way past her and get out. Just *go*!

"Are you a drowned rat? That's what you look like." That awful chortle again and Crazy Mary tossed a frayed blanket at Lizabeth. "Here."

Lizabeth caught it automatically. It smelled, but she couldn't resist wrapping it around her wet and freezing body. She was uncertain. Outside was the driving rain. Inside was Crazy Mary! Though Kat's father said she was harmless . . . No, of course she couldn't *stay* here!

"Six years," Crazy Mary mumbled. "No one remembers the *North Star*. You don't know. You don't know anything."

"The *North Star*?" Lizabeth repeated. She had been seven when the shock and sadness of it affected the whole town.

"What do *you* know?" Crazy Mary sounded belligerent and Lizabeth shrank back.

"I remember the *North Star*," Lizabeth said. "It sank."

"It took all four with it. To the bottom of the sea. Down to the crabs and the lobsters and the creeping crawlers and—"

"Eight men went down with the North Star," Lizabeth corrected. This *was* crazy! Was she actually having a conversation of sorts with Crazy Mary? But if she kept the old woman calm and talking . . . She'd make her move soon, suddenly brush past her. Lizabeth shuddered. Back into the rain with no place to go.

"Four of mine," Crazy Mary said. "John Dellrow. My husband. He was fifty-six. Fifty-six is too soon, don't you think? Johnny Dellrow, Jr. He was thirty, the image of his father. A fine boy. Oh, he hated it when they called him Junior. Alan Dellrow, twenty-eight. Alan always said fishing was no kind of life. Not tough enough for it. Wanted to work on a farm. I'll tell you the truth: John had no patience for him."

Lizabeth had never connected the Dellrow tragedy with Crazy Mary. "I'm sorry," she said.

Crazy Mary didn't seem to hear her. Her talk flowed out as if a dam had opened.

"Alan, well, he was the one remembered flowers on my birthday. Daffodils one year, tied up with a yellow ribbon. Now wasn't that nice? Imagine, flowers on my birthday! And Kevin, just turned fifteen. He was the baby. Didn't think I'd have another one, but then there was Kevin. He was my special one. Knew his numbers and letters and such a smile! I didn't want him going out with the others that day." Crazy Mary groaned. "I said he oughta be in school. But he wanted to be a man like his brothers. You should have seen his eyes, begging to go. John said I was babying him, making him soft. John was head of the house, you know, so I said all right. I had an awful cold feeling that day, but I said all right. That's what I did. And I started the codfish stew for dinner, cutting up onions and all. Potatoes, too. Had plenty of potatoes in those days."

"I'm sorry," Lizabeth repeated. Pity had almost replaced her fear.

"What do *you* know? I waited at the dock. September fourteenth, 1900. I waited and waited. The other boats came in and I waited. What do you know about grief?"

"Nothing, but . . ." Lizabeth took a breath. "My little sister has scarlet fever. Tracy. She's only four. Tonight she was saying things. Things that didn't make sense. What does that mean?"

"*Pshaw*! What makes sense and what don't? Makes no difference." Crazy Mary laughed. "I don't give two figs for sense."

"I'm scared for her," Lizabeth said. She was talking only to herself now. "I'm scared."

"You're a young one. Are you a friend to my Kevin?"

"No, I'm sorry, I don't know Kevin."

"He's the one with the nice smile. The girls are crazy for him. You know who I mean? The one with the dimples. You can't miss him."

"I don't know him."

Crazy Mary stared at Lizabeth. "What's your mother think, sending you out like that? Barefoot and a ripped-up dress! Hair like a rat's nest. I don't send my boys out like that!"

Lizabeth shrugged.

"I'm turning in," Crazy Mary said, "I have my rounds to make first thing in the morning. You can stay, but if you make any noise I'm sending you right out in the storm. No shenanigans, mark my word!"

"Yes, Mrs. Dellrow."

"They call me Mary," she mumbled.

Lizabeth took a far corner and rested on the floor against the wall. The blanket smelled terrible, but it kept her warm.

❧

"Wake up if you want to eat!" Mary nudged Lizabeth with her toe. "Don't think I'm serving breakfast in bed."

Lizabeth couldn't believe that she had managed to sleep—and with Crazy Mary nearby—but light was now seeping around the edges of the door. It was morning!

"Shake a leg. I'm hungry," Mary said.

Lizabeth's stomach was grumbling. She had hardly eaten the chicken at Kat's last night. Now she'd give anything for a piece of it. She wondered what Mary did for food.

The old woman beckoned impatiently. Lizabeth combed her fingers through her hair and followed Mary out of the hut.

It was just dawn. The chill of the night was already gone. It would be an unseasonably warm May day. Lizabeth's clothes were still wet, and she was grateful to feel the first rays of the sun.

Lizabeth followed Mary along Wharf Way. She was still barefoot and limping, but her heel didn't hurt as much anymore. She felt so much better. A night of sleep had healed her. We Merchant girls, she thought, we recover fast. Tracy, too, would be better this morning.

They passed the bustling docks. They were full of activity: men loading boats, calling to each other, hoisting sails.

In contrast, Lighthouse Lane was sleepy and deserted at this early hour. Mary loped along toward the center of town and Lizabeth followed, puzzled. They reached the village green. The stores around the square were still closed.

"Quick before they spot us," Mary said. "Got a late start this morning!"

She led Lizabeth behind the bakery on East Street, where waste bins were lined up in the alley.

"He throws out stale things," Mary said. "The best pickings are in here." She waded into the garbage.

No, I'm not eating *garbage*, Lizabeth thought. But she was so hungry. The tantalizing aromas from the back door of the bakery made her mouth water. Mr. Witherspoon must be at the ovens now, she thought, preparing the day's goods.

If I'm going to eat today, Lizabeth thought, maybe this is it. Maybe I have to. How quickly life could change!

Then she noticed that Mary had taken a paper-wrapped packet from the top of the bin. Who *wraps* garbage? It contained three rolls.

"No doughnuts," Mary grumbled. "On good days, I find a doughnut."

When Mary offered Lizabeth a roll, she took it, hesitated for just a moment, and bit in.

The roll wasn't stale at all. The caraway-sprinkled crust was crisp, the inside was soft, and Lizabeth suspected it was still warm from the oven. Lizabeth was sure Mr. Witherspoon had put it out especially for Mary, even if she didn't realize that.

The same thing happened when they explored the

garbage behind the general store. A carefully covered wedge of cheddar was waiting on top. Lizabeth broke off a piece. It tasted fresh from the wheel in the store. Cranky old Mr. Thomas must have been thinking of Mary, too. The people of Cape Light were so kind!

Mary gummed the cheese with smacking sounds. She dismissed Lizabeth with a wave of her hand. "Go on your way now. I have things to do."

"Thank you," Lizabeth said, "for everything."

Mary didn't answer. Lizabeth watched the old woman shuffle down the alley in her torn, oversized shoes. A last glimpse of flying, disheveled gray hair, and Mary disappeared around a corner.

Lizabeth wandered toward the village green. She saw Mr. Hardy unlocking the door of the telegraph office. Cape Light was coming to life. If anyone noticed her barefoot and ragged, there'd be questions to answer. Someone would surely tell her parents. She'd have to stay out of sight. After dark she would go to see Tracy again. What could she do until evening?

It was a long and lonely day. Lizabeth walked aimlessly on a little-used road in the direction of Potter's Orchard, but the sound of a horse and carriage made her duck behind a briar bush. After it was safely past, she headed the other way toward Durham Point. She went by the salt marsh. She was walking in circles. Hours must have passed. The sun was high in the sky now. Her clothes were almost dry.

Hunger told her that it had to be lunchtime.

Lizabeth sat down on an old pine trunk felled by a long-ago storm. It was crumbly and covered with lichens. Twittering birds were loud. Nuthatches? Chickadees? She didn't know one bird call from another. Even the birds had each other for company, she thought. She had no one.

Another day of my walkabout, she thought. No one to meet but myself. Hello Lizabeth, this is who you are. Food, shelter, family, and friends are all you need. This is what's real. The girl who pretended to be dumb and got into knots over a beauty event and complained about lighthouse discomforts was gone, someone she hardly remembered.

She was so hungry! She dreamed of roast beef and lemon meringue pie, and her mouth watered. Any kind of food would do. A crust of bread, anything. She decided to chance going into town to see what she could forage.

At the town square she kept to the shadows in the back alleys.

"Lizabeth! Lizabeth!" It was Kat's voice calling from the street. She sounded tearful. "I didn't mean anything I said. Not a word! Lizabeth, if you can hear me . . ."

"Lizabeth!" Amanda called. "Lizabeth, where are you?"

They were looking for her! And poor Kat thought she'd disappeared because of their fight. She wanted to reassure her. She wanted so badly to run to them!

No, she couldn't! Kat and Amanda might tell Mother and Father. She couldn't blame them. When Kat had stowed away to Boston last year, Lizabeth had broken her promise not to tell because she thought Kat was in danger. She'd thought it was the right thing to do. Kat and Amanda might feel the same way.

Lizabeth couldn't let anything stop her from seeing Tracy tonight. She *had* to see Tracy no matter what! So she hid behind a barrel in the alley until Kat's and Amanda's voices faded away toward North Street. And she was left twice as lonely.

She found nothing in the bins but half a wormy peach and a slice of bread green with mildew. She gagged. All right; she'd go hungry today. One day wasn't that long.

When it was twilight, Lizabeth crept back to the

village green. There were only a few stragglers left. She saw Mr. Thomas lock up the general store. The old men had deserted the bench in front of the courthouse. She'd sit there and wait until it was dark enough to climb the trellis. Soon . . .

She was crossing the green when she saw two familiar figures. Chris and Rose! Together—and holding hands! Lizabeth ducked behind the statue of the lost fisherman. She peeked out at them.

Chris and Rose went to the bench and sat down. And then—Lizabeth couldn't believe her eyes! Chris sat slumped with his head in his hands. His shoulders were shaking. Rose had a comforting arm around him.

He was *crying*! Impossible. Boys and men didn't cry. Chris certainly *never* cried. But that's what she was seeing. Something must have happened. Something terrible. Tracy!

~thirteen~

L izabeth ran to Rose and Chris.

"Tracy? What is it? What happened?" she asked.

Chris and Rose looked up, startled. "Nothing," Chris mumbled.

"You were *crying*!" Lizabeth said.

Chris looked furious and embarrassed. "She's my little sister, too, you know."

"Where were you? We were all looking for you," Rose said. "Your aunt didn't have the heart to tell your mother. Not when she's so worried about—"

"What happened to you?" Chris seem shocked at her appearance. "Where are your shoes?"

"What did you hear about Tracy?" Lizabeth interrupted.

Rose reached for Lizabeth's hand. "She's not doing well."

Chris's voice was ragged. "Dr. Forbes says it's critical."

Lizabeth gasped. "I saw her last night and she—"

"How did you see her? The quarantine . . ." Chris said.

"I sneaked in last night and the night before," Lizabeth told them. "I *had* to! I'm just waiting for dark to go back."

Chris wiped his eyes roughly. "And you exposed yourself? I've been wanting to see her, I've thought of nothing else—didn't you give a thought to Mother and Father? If you catch it, too . . ."

"I *had* to—" Lizabeth repeated.

"Of all the stupid—" he started.

"Leave her alone," Rose's eyes were sad and gentle. "She feels as bad as you do."

"Well, you don't have to sneak in tonight," Chris said. "You can go in the front door."

"I can't. They'll send me away to Pittsfield."

"You've been exposed already! You think they'll send you to infect our uncle and aunt?"

"Oh," Lizabeth said. "I never thought of that."

"You never thought at all." Chris sounded both angry and miserable. "You picked a great time to go missing!"

"How . . . how bad is Tracy?" Lizabeth asked.

"Bad," Chris said.

"Oh, Chris," Rose said. "There's always hope."

Her big brother had been *crying*! Lizabeth was terrified. She ran all the way home and burst through the front door. Mother, Father, and Dr. Forbes met her in the hallway. They stared at her, shocked.

"Lizabeth! You can't come in!" Mother's eyes were red and swollen.

"What are you doing? Go back to the lighthouse!" Though Father was shouting, he couldn't hide the fear in his voice. "Immediately!"

"I'm here to see Tracy. How is she? I need to see her."

"Don't you understand?" Mother said. "She's *contagious*."

"I've *been* with her. Last night and the night before. So it doesn't matter anymore, does it? Let me see her. *Please*."

"Not you, too," Mother moaned. "I can't stand it." She held a glass of water, her hand shaking so that it threatened to spill. She looked at Dr. Forbes.

"If Lizabeth was already in Tracy's room," Dr. Forbes said slowly, "I suppose she could. . . . Under the circumstances . . ." He looked exhausted.

"She's been calling for you," Father said. "Maybe seeing her sister . . ."

"I . . . I was just taking this up," Mother said.

"I'll take it." Lizabeth grabbed the glass. She hurried to the stairs before anyone could change their mind. She wanted to run, but the water forced her to move slowly.

Halfway up, she heard Father roaring at Dr. Forbes. "Can't you do *something*? Try leeches! Remove the bad blood." He was so used to being in control.

"I don't believe in leeches, Mr. Merchant." Dr. Forbes said quietly. "I won't torment her."

"Do *something*!" Father raged in his helplessness.

"Stanton, please," Mother sobbed.

"The only thing is to keep her hydrated and comfortable," Dr. Forbes said. "We have to wait. We have to hope the fever will break by morning."

Lizabeth felt Father's rage. Why wasn't there medicine for scarlet fever? *Why*? It was 1906! New things were being discovered all the time!

She entered Tracy's room. Tracy looked so terribly flushed against the white sheets.

"Tracy?"

"Lillibet," Tracy whispered her long-ago baby pronunciation. Her voice was just a breath. Lizabeth had to bend over to hear. "You came back."

"I'm here." She wasn't delirious! She wasn't! That had to mean she was better.

"I knew you would come back," Tracy whispered. "I waited for you."

"Do you want water?" Lizabeth asked. "See, I brought some up for you."

Tracy shook her head slowly. She seemed too weak to even do that much. But her dark blue eyes were aware. Tracy was back from that faraway place!

"Just a sip?"

"No, no more," Tracy sighed.

"Maybe a little later." With her finger, Lizabeth placed a drop on the parched lips and rested the glass on the nightstand.

Tracy's lips flickered into the trace of a smile. "I knew you'd come back."

"Nothing could keep me away," Lizabeth said. "Nothing in the whole world."

Tracy moaned. "I'm hot and then I'm shivery and then I'm hot."

"Oh, I know." Please, God, she's only a little girl!

"Lillibet," Tracy whispered, "stay with me."

"I will," Lizabeth promised. "I love you, pussycat."

She took Tracy's tiny hand. "I love you."

Tracy's eyelids fluttered closed.

There was another sigh; a deep sigh that seemed to rattle Tracy's small body. Her hand suddenly went limp in Lizabeth's.

"Tracy." Lizabeth shook her arm. "Tracy, wake up." Over and over again, she repeated, "Tracy. No, Tracy, come back. *Tracy!*"

But she knew, as surely as she knew anything, that she had just seen Tracy's spirit escape.

"Mother! Mother!" someone screamed. "Mother!" It was a while before Lizabeth realized it was her own voice.

⚘fourteen⚘

Lizabeth stumbled on the stone steps in front of the church. If Father hadn't been holding her arm, she would have fallen.

The church was a simple white clapboard building that, except for the spire, blended into its surroundings. Inside, plain white walls surrounded rows of oak benches. Their armrests had been lovingly hand-carved by parishioners, with no two designs alike. This was the place where Lizabeth had always felt peace and harmony.

Tall windows gave an impression of airiness. In winter the snow outside reflected light into the long, narrow room. Today, on this nineteenth day of May, soft sunlight shone through the glass.

The many empty pews were obvious. People were afraid to gather in large groups.

Lizabeth allowed Father to guide her to a seat next to Mother. There was no peace and harmony here today.

There was a small white casket. It was terribly wrong, Lizabeth thought. Such a small casket was an insult to the order of the world. It was covered with white lilies. Their heavy scent became nauseating.

Reverend Morgan spoke. Lizabeth watched his lips move. She couldn't take in his words. She was numb. Everything seemed to click by like disconnected slides in a stereoscope.

The too-tight unfamiliar black crepe dress.

Ada's round tear-stained face at the back of the church.

Father's sobs. "Such a short time. I wish I'd—" He had aged overnight. "We had her for such a short time."

Mother, deathly still in the pew next to him, her face white and haunted.

Her friends on the stone steps outside. Amanda, Kat, and Rose. Their painful, awkward silence. Kat saying, "You know I loved her, too." Rose saying, "I'm so sorry." Amanda's hug, tears in Amanda's eyes. "I know, oh Lizabeth, I know."

Lizabeth didn't cry. She didn't speak. She was numb.

The gravesite. "Ashes to ashes and dust to dust." Reverend Morgan's anguished eyes.

She and Christopher, clutching each other's hands,

brother and sister as lost as Hansel and Gretel trying to find a path home.

Chill winds blew into the wide open windows of Lizabeth's house. They were airing out, grimly following Dr. Forbes's instructions. He thought scarlet fever came from airborne germs, though no one knew for sure. They burned Tracy's bedclothes. Lizabeth hated all of it, hated the feeling that they were dispersing the last bits of Tracy.

Later a sprinkling of neighbors and friends came into the parlor. Others, still afraid to enter the Merchant house, left offerings on the porch. Covered dishes, more than an army could ever need. Then, finally, quiet. Lizabeth, Chris, Mother, and Father sat at the table over untouched food. Tracy's chair was empty.

When Lizabeth went up the stairs to bed, Father was still sitting at the table, staring hopelessly into space.

The sleep that overwhelmed Lizabeth was welcome. She burrowed into its dark, unthinking depth.

Lizabeth woke up in her own lavender-and-white room, on her own smooth sheets, with a sigh of pleasure. She stretched comfortably. It felt as though she'd been away for a long time. . . .

"Lizabeth! Lizabeth! I'm ready!" Tracy's excited voice preceded her down the hall, and soon she burst through Lizabeth's door.

Lizabeth smiled. Tracy's curls still needed brushing and the red bow perched on her head was crooked, but she looked so sweet in the navy-and-red plaid dress. Navy tights, patent high-button shoes, a white eyelet pinafore that allowed the plaid of the dress to peep through. Adorable! They'd been planning this first-day-of-school outfit together for days.

"It's *very* early," Lizabeth said. She sat up and swung her feet unto the floor. Her head felt foggy. She had a hazy memory of a bad dream. It had faded away with the morning light. "Can you stay neat while I get dressed?"

Tracy nodded eagerly. Then a frown appeared between her big, dark blue eyes. "I don't want to be late."

"Don't worry." Lizabeth laughed. "I promise you, the William McKinley School won't be open for more than an hour."

"I'm glad you still go there." Tracy beamed. "I'm glad you're taking me."

For a moment Lizabeth was confused. Of course, she had just come out of a deep sleep. . . . Tracy was six and starting first grade today. So Lizabeth had to be fifteen and in ninth grade. . . . Of course. When she'd swung her feet over the side of her bed, her legs had been noticeably longer. Yes, she'd graduate from William McKinley next spring and go on to high school in Cranberry. Why was it so hard to keep track of dates? September 1908 already!

Tracy and Lizabeth walked along Lighthouse Lane and turned the corner to William McKinley Road. Well, Lizabeth was walking. Tracy, holding tight to her hand, skipped along.

Mothers and big brothers and sisters were going the same way, bringing other first graders to their first day of school. Some of the little children looked scared. Some were whimpering. One little girl stood still on the sidewalk, bawling. Her mother tried to guide her along, but she pulled back and refused to move. "Come now, Evangeline," the mother said. "Everyone's going to school. You'll like it." She pointed at Tracy going by. "Look at that little girl. See how happy she is?"

Tracy gave Lizabeth a big smile. "*I'm* not scared," she said.

Lizabeth smiled back. "I know you're not." Pride in Tracy filled her heart. Her little sister was so full of confidence, so brimming over with joy. What a special six-year-old she was!

"I know how to read 'cat' and 'hat' and 'mat,'" Tracy said.

Lizabeth nodded. Tracy would do well at William McKinley. She was so bright—Lizabeth was sure she was way ahead for her age—and cheerful and outgoing. Everyone would love her.

The sunshine was turning Tracy's golden curls into a halo. "Thanks for walking me."

"I wouldn't miss it for anything," Lizabeth said. "I love you, pussycat."

Then, like a cloud passing over, Lizabeth remembered her nightmare. It was still hazy. Something about illness. Scarlet fever. Father crying. *Father?* That was unimaginable! Tracy, burning with fever and suddenly so still. No, no, that was too horrible.

Lizabeth shook her head, shook away the images. Tracy would do beautifully in school and grow up and fall in love one day, and they'd whisper confidences and giggle like sisters do. Tracy might even have an outstanding talent. . . . Maybe piano, maybe art like Kat, or . . . There were endless possibilities.

What a cruel nightmare! The sadness of it seeped

into Lizabeth's bones and made her body feel heavy. Some part of her had lived within that horror all through the night. But now it was daylight and the Indian summer sunshine warmed Lizabeth. Thank God, *this* was reality! Lizabeth breathed deep. Thank you, God. Tracy's little hand was in hers. Lizabeth squeezed it and—

Lizabeth woke up in her own lavender-and-white room on her own smooth sheets. Her bedside clock read nine o'clock. She was confused. Oh, no! She must have overslept. She was supposed to walk Tracy to school!

"Tracy!" she called.

Lizabeth bounded out of bed and her eye caught the black crepe mourning dress draped over a chair. She caught her breath.

"Tracy," she whimpered.

Lizabeth doubled over in pain. It was the nightmare that was real! It was like losing Tracy a second time. Worse because there had been that sweet, fleeting dream of how it should have been.

⌘ *fifteen* ⌘

The only thing Lizabeth could hold on to for comfort was that she'd had the chance to tell Tracy she loved her. It mattered.

Late the next day, after more neighbors with hot dishes had come and gone, Lizabeth saw Chris sitting on the porch rocker in the twilight. His shoulders were slumped forward. She came out and sat on the wicker chair across from him. He looked up at her and then away. They sat in silence, staring out at the darkening evening.

"Chris . . ." Lizabeth said.

He turned to her. His face, in the light from the gas lamp, was full of sadness. "It's not real to me. I can't get it into my mind."

"I know."

They listened to a far-off train whistle.

"Chris, I love you," Lizabeth said. She felt terribly

awkward. "I just wanted to tell you. Out loud. I was thinking about the things we never say to each other—"

"In this family," he finished her thought. His voice softened. "I love you, too."

"We're getting older now," Lizabeth said. "We should stop sniping at each other."

Chris nodded. "I'm not a kid anymore." He shifted in his chair. "Everything's different."

"I know brothers and sisters tease and fight, but . . ."

"We have nothing to fight about," he said. "It seems stupid now, doesn't it? I remember when you were born. I remember being glad I wasn't outnumbered by the grown-ups anymore."

"I remember when Tracy was born. I was so happy there was another girl." Lizabeth remembered the rest of it: her thudding disappointment when she saw the red-faced, bald, bawling infant. It took her a while to truly love Tracy.

Chris sighed.

They sat together thinking. The runners of the rocker squealed under Chris.

"Lizabeth? When it comes down to it, you know you can always depend on me."

"I know."

"No reason we can't get along. We never gave credit to how much we have in common." He mustered that crooked grin, the grin that she couldn't help being charmed by, even when she was furious at him. "Look, we even share the same best friend."

"Your best friend?" Lizabeth asked, puzzled. She hardly knew Michael Potter.

"Rose."

"Oh!" Rose and Chris, best friends! "Do you . . . I mean, do you like her as a *girl*?"

"That, too," Chris said.

"Are you—are you two a *couple*?"

"If she'll have me," he said quietly.

Lizabeth was astounded. She had never ever heard him sound so *humble*. This was brashly confident Chris, a great catch—and he'd always acted like he knew it. He could charm anyone, and half the girls in town had set their caps for him. And it was *Rose*!

"She's sweet and fun and . . ." Lizabeth started.

"You don't have to tell me. She's . . . well, she's *everything*!" For a moment, his face lit up.

Rose, who doesn't follow the rules in the *Girls' Guides* and the *Ladies' Home Journal*, Lizabeth thought. Rose, who is always just herself.

"Father was out here a little while ago," Chris said. "It was peculiar. He asked me how I felt about things, why I wouldn't work in the bank, what I wanted to do instead. Even what I thought of the high school! Trying to get acquainted all of a sudden. It was the first time he *listened* to me."

"He's trying," Lizabeth said. She had been touched by Father's awkward attempts at affection.

"Too late," Chris said. "He missed out on knowing his own daughter."

"There's a big hole in this family now," Lizabeth said. Two out of three was a lonely number.

⚘

To her surprise, Lizabeth didn't get sick. No sign of fever. Not even a sniffle from her walkabout in the rain. She went to Dr. Forbes's office to be checked anyway because Mother asked her to. Mother was suddenly so frail and helpless. Lizabeth couldn't refuse her anything.

Lizabeth sat on the examining table in Dr. Forbes' office and looked around at all the shiny equipment and instruments and pill bottles. All those things and nothing had saved Tracy.

"I don't know why one person catches scarlet fever

and another doesn't." Dr. Forbes put his stethoscope aside. "Some people have resistance. You're lucky. You seem to have some kind of natural immunity."

Lizabeth couldn't feel lucky.

"Couldn't *something* have helped my sister?" she asked. "If we'd realized she was getting sick sooner. If we'd been in New York? Maybe in a big city or . . ."

Dr. Forbes shook his head. "Don't, Lizabeth." His long days and nights showed on his drawn face. "There is no cure for scarlet fever. Not anywhere; not yet. With all we've learned, we still depend on the body to heal itself."

"You said not *yet*," Lizabeth said.

"Because I have hope. Medicine has come a long way."

"Has it?"

"At least now we know that sanitation is important. It wasn't that long ago that surgeons didn't even wash their hands. I have to believe that someday there'll be a treatment, a drug for scarlet fever, cholera, diphtheria, tuberculosis. . . ." His voice trailed off.

"A miracle drug?" Lizabeth asked in disbelief.

"If not in my lifetime, perhaps in yours."

"Too late for Tracy," Lizabeth said bitterly.

"But not for other children." He drew a weary hand across his forehead. "I pray for the day when a doctor can do more than look wise and reassuring." With an effort, he straightened his shoulders. "We *have* made progress."

How terrible it must be for him, Lizabeth thought, to lose another patient. But he keeps on trying. She looked at his graying beard and metal-framed spectacles. How does he do it, she wondered. He's some kind of hero.

❧

When Lizabeth came home she found Mother straightening up the kitchen with Ada's apron wrapped around her. The servants hadn't returned to the Merchant house yet.

The lady with the sparkling jewels, elaborate hairstyle, and easy smile had disappeared, Lizabeth thought.

"What are we going to do with all of this?" Mother put yet another covered dish in the icebox. "Do people really think *food* will help?"

"They don't know what else to do," Lizabeth said.

"I suppose it's meant as a reminder to keep on living." Mother's mouth twisted. "They don't know."

They know, Lizabeth thought. We're not the only ones.

"We'll never eat all of this," Mother said, "but it seems wrong to throw it out." She sighed.

"Wait, I know what to do with it!" Lizabeth juggled two full bowls out of the crowded icebox and put them on the counter. A chicken mixture with a crust of crumbs, and baked fish and potatoes. "I know someone who'll want it. Oh, and I have to get something else!" She ran upstairs and found an extra blanket in the back of the linen closet. Light blue, soft wool. It won't stay clean and sweet-smelling for long, Lizabeth thought, but it will be warm.

"Where did that blanket come from?" Mother shook her head. "I don't remember it."

"We don't need it, do we?" Lizabeth gathered everything together.

"Where are you going? What's this all about?"

"There's something I have to do." Mother wouldn't want to know about that night. Lizabeth wasn't ready to tell even Amanda, Kat, and Rose yet. It was too strange and unreal.

She managed to get the bulky bowls into the basket of her bicycle. She draped the blanket over the handlebars. Lizabeth rode slowly along Lighthouse Lane. The extra weight made the bicycle lopsided. At every bump, she put a protective hand over the basket.

She turned onto Wharf Way and came to the tumble-down hut. In daylight, it was horribly shabby: the door hanging from its hinges, broken and weather-beaten planks, shredded wood.

Lizabeth carried the bowls and the blanket into the hut. Mary was out. She placed everything on the crate next to the candles. Mary would be so surprised by this sudden windfall.

She didn't have to know where it came from.

For the first time since Tracy's death, Lizabeth felt good about something.

✌✌

Amanda, Kat, and Rose rallied around Lizabeth. Sometimes it was all three of them together. At least one of them was always with Lizabeth, though Kat had light-house chores, Rose had duties at the stables, and Amanda had Hannah. Lizabeth was never alone. They seemed to have planned it that way, taking turns.

The best friends anyone could have, Lizabeth thought.

Kat and Rose did all they could to comfort her and Lizabeth was grateful. But she could speak most freely to Amanda, who knew all about loss.

"I don't know what to do," Lizabeth told Amanda. "I

don't know how to stop being so sad."

They were at Amanda's house that afternoon because she had to be at home for Hannah. Amanda had started Hannah on cutting out paper dolls in her room. Then she and Lizabeth settled into Amanda's room. They sat side by side on the bed.

"Does it ever get better? Do you ever get over it?" Lizabeth pleaded.

"You don't really get over it." Amanda said slowly. "I never stop missing my mother. I choose a new dress or some little thing happens on an ordinary day—even something funny—I *ache* with wanting to tell her, and suddenly a stab of hurt takes my breath away." She twisted the chenille bedspread in her hand. "I want to tell her about Jed. I want to show her my report card when I get an A. Especially now that I'm older, I want to ask her about womanly things. And it's not Rose's mother or Kat's mother or yours that I want, though they've been so kind to me. I want my *own*."

"Then you stay sad forever." Lizabeth felt hopeless.

"No, it does get better. One day you remember how magnificent God's world is. I was in the lighthouse tower with Kat at sunset. For a moment the sea and the sky turned red and orange and pink, and all that beauty seemed like a . . . like a message for me. Then I knew I'd be all right. You don't forget, Lizabeth, but you start to enjoy all the good things again. Give yourself time."

Hannah burst into the room almost in tears. "I cut the tab off by mistake. The coat won't stay on!"

"Let me see," Amanda said. She took the little blue paper coat from Hannah and bent the shoulder. "I'm bending it just a tiny bit. It won't show." She folded it onto the cardboard Gibson Girl. "Look, it stays on."

"It shows!" Hannah exploded. "It does too show. The shoulder looks all funny!"

"But it still looks pretty on her."

"No, it doesn't! You spoiled it!"

"Look at all those pretty buttons, Hannah-banana. See if you can find the matching hat and cut it out *very* carefully."

Hannah pouted and grumbled her way out of the room.

"I would have said 'Don't yell at *me*, it's not *my* fault if you messed up the tab.'" Lizabeth half-smiled. "Mean old me. You're awfully patient."

"She has no one but me." Amanda sighed. "Anyway, Hannah's irritable because she can't play with Mary Margaret today. She's usually a sweetheart."

Why wasn't I more patient with Tracy? Lizabeth thought. *Why?* She cleared the sudden thickness in her throat. "It's terribly hard for you, isn't it? Hannah *and* running the household."

"I don't mind."

"I've never once heard you complain, but still—"

"We do have a laundress come in and—I want to raise Hannah right and keep a nice home for my father. Honestly, I *want* to. After my mother . . . Well, it was good for me to be busy with something outside myself. It helps." Amanda hesitated before she added, "I like to think my mother would be proud of me."

"You know she would!"

"I want to make my father proud, too. I wish he had more time with us. He used to be home lots of evenings before. But of course, he's doing important work, counseling and . . ."

"Everyone admires him," Lizabeth said. "They say he's the best minister Cape Light could have, always available for anyone who's troubled. But don't you ever tell him? I mean, that you and Hannah need him, too?"

"I can't." A frown crossed Amanda's forehead. "I think he's driven to keep busy and lose himself in good works. Sometimes I think he's stuck in his grief." She clapped her hand over her mouth. "Don't tell anyone I said that. Don't ever repeat it!"

"I won't," Lizabeth promised. She'd never noticed before; beautiful Amanda's nails were bitten and ragged.

"I didn't mean it," Amanda said quickly. "I'm lucky to have a father I respect so much. I hope to be worthy of him."

Stuck in grief, Lizabeth thought. I don't want to be like that, but I don't know *how* to go on.

⚜sixteen⚜

It was the middle of June and the roses were in full bloom now, all over town. The cream and pink flowers were especially lush on the trellis in front of Lizabeth's house. There were no blooms on the side trellis. Lizabeth must have knocked off the buds when she climbed up on those terrible nights.

Kat, Rose, and Amanda invented things to do to lure Lizabeth out of her room.

"Come on, Lizabeth, let's go to the lighthouse," Kat said.

"We can have a picnic on the rocks," Rose said.

Amanda took her hand. "It's good for you to get out and be with your friends."

Lizabeth walked down Lighthouse Lane with them. Orange daylilies grew wild along the sides of the road. Pansies, phlox, and delphiniums brightened cottage gardens. Lizabeth averted her eyes from the glorious, hateful colors. Everything beautiful, everything growing in its own season. Except for Tracy. Lizabeth was ashamed of her urge to pull the flowers up by their roots. She understood why Mary Dellrow did that.

As if the thought of Mary had made her appear, there she was. She was walking in the opposite direction on Lighthouse Lane, toward them. Kat, Rose, and Amanda edged to the far side of the road, partway into the underbrush to get out of her path.

Rose tugged at Lizabeth. "Come on, hurry out of her way!"

Lizabeth stood still and stared. There was something way off about Mary today, even more than usual. She wore a bedraggled feathered hat that must have been discarded somewhere. Strands of her long gray hair were tied with multicolored ribbons. A wilted daisy was pinned to the lapel of her red satin jacket. The shiny fabric was badly ripped along the side. One sleeve was missing and the other hung by a thread. She walked along jauntily in spite of her oversized shoes. She was the picture of festivity gone bizarre.

Lizabeth started toward her.

"Lizabeth, that's *Crazy Mary*!" Amanda exclaimed.

"Her name is Mary Dellrow. Mrs. Dellrow." Lizabeth

shook off Kat's restraining hand.

"Lizabeth, what are you *doing*?" Rose asked.

"I know her." Lizabeth said, and took another step forward. Out of the corner of her eye she saw her friends' shocked faces.

As she approached Mary, the woman's eyes widened and she quickly backed away. She's *afraid*, Lizabeth thought.

"Let me be," the woman quavered. "Leave me alone."

"It's me. Lizabeth."

Mary peered at her suspiciously and finally there was the spark of recognition. "Well, aren't *you* fancy today! Where'd you find those? Didn't know you in your fancy getup!" Feathers drooped over her forehead. "So you're going, too, eh? All spiffy and fine."

"Going where?" Lizabeth asked.

"To the *graduation*. Where do you think? Graduation day in Cranberry! My Kevin, first one in the family to finish the high school." Her chin lifted with pride. "I told you he was the smart one, didn't I?"

Lizabeth's heart sank. "Mary, don't go to Cranberry." The high school graduation *was* scheduled for today. She must have heard. . . .

"Wild horses can't keep me away! Get a move on, we can't be late." She chuckled. "Good thing you're not a drowned rat today."

"Kevin isn't graduating today," Lizabeth said gently. She didn't know what to do, but she *couldn't* let Mary go all the way to Cranberry and burst into the ceremony. It would be so much worse for her.

"What are you saying, girl? Speak up!"

"I'm sorry, I'm so sorry, Kevin isn't . . . Mary, your Kevin is gone."

"My Kevin? Gone? Gone where?" Four heartbeats went by and then Mary's face crumpled with realization. It was painful for Lizabeth to watch.

"Gone to the bottom of the sea," Mary moaned.

"I'm sorry," Lizabeth said. "I know how it is."

Mary tore off the daisy and threw it furiously on the road. Her entire body slumped as she slowly turned back toward Wharf Way.

"Mary, wait! What happened to your arm?" The sleeveless arm was swollen and angry red from her wrist almost to her elbow.

"Nothing happened," Mary muttered. "A nail in the bin hooked me."

"You've got to do something. It looks bad!"

"It don't hurt that much," Mary said. "Not that much."

"You should see a doctor."

"No! No doctors! I don't see 'em and they don't see me."

Amanda and Rose, with Kat in the lead, had stepped closer. They formed a loose semicircle around Lizabeth and looked on, surprised and curious. They raised questioning eyebrows.

"I'll tell you about it sometime," Lizabeth promised.

She wasn't ready to talk about that night yet. "First, someone needs to take care of that arm."

"That old sawbones in Cranberry ain't touching me. He'll whack it off!" Mary began to shuffle away.

"We have a new doctor, right here in Cape Light," Lizabeth followed her footsteps. "Dr. Forbes. All the way from New York City! I'll take you. . . ."

"No! Stop bothering me."

Lizabeth mouthed a silent "help me" to her friends.

Mary looked at the other girls in alarm as they came close. "Leave me alone, you!" She shrank back. "Go away."

"It's all right," Lizabeth said. "This is Kat Williams from the lighthouse. You know her, don't you? Tom Williams's daughter?"

Mary squinted. "The Williams girl?"

"And the *minister's* daughter, Amanda." That had to make Mary feel safer. "And Dr. Forbes is Rose's father."

Rose stepped up. "My father will know how to help you. He's very good, honestly." And then to Lizabeth, "He should be in the office now, just finishing office hours."

"Come, Mary, before he leaves. We'll all go with you," Lizabeth said. "He's right on Lighthouse Lane."

It took all four together, with Kat's best powers of persuasion and Amanda's soft, soothing tone, to keep Mary moving toward the Forbes house. Rose walked just behind them, which stopped the skittish woman from turning back. It was about as easy, Lizabeth thought, as herding cats.

They finally reached Rose's house and found Dr. Forbes in the waiting room. Lizabeth had to give him credit. He quickly covered his astonishment at Mary's grotesque finery and immediately focused on her arm.

"It's badly infected. It's a good thing you came in."

Mary grunted.

"Here's what we'll do." He spoke directly to Mary as though she was a normal patient. "I have to lance it and I'm sorry, it *will* hurt. But then, I promise you, you'll feel much better. It's throbbing now, isn't it?"

Mary nodded.

"When the infection is cleaned out, I'll bandage the wound and it'll have a chance to heal. Is that all right with you?"

Mary looked longingly back at the door. Lizabeth touched her shoulder.

"You'll have trouble if you neglect it," Dr. Forbes said. "Please, come into the office."

"I can't pay you money," Mary told him. She gave him a shrewd squint. "I can give you a lobster cage, hardly used."

Dr. Forbes covered the beginning of a smile with a serious expression and said, "Very well, Mrs. Dellrow. That will do nicely." He turned to the girls. "One of you has to hold her arm for me."

"I will," Lizabeth volunteered. Mary trusted her the most.

"Lizabeth, are you sure you can?" Kat asked. Of course, her cousin must be thinking of how squeamish she had always been.

Lizabeth nodded. She left her friends in the waiting room and guided the hesitant woman into Dr. Forbes's office.

"Hold her arm steady for me, at the wrist and at the elbow," Dr. Forbes directed. He took a shining knifelike instrument from his cabinet. "Take a deep breath," he told Mary just before he made the cut. Lizabeth took a deep breath, too.

The blade cut into the bulging, swollen flesh. In spite of herself, Lizabeth was fascinated by the calm competence and precision of his actions. Then he pressed two spots on Mary's arm and pus came rushing out. Streams of yellow pus mixed with streaks of blood! Lizabeth should have been disgusted but instead she was amazed at how he knew exactly where to press. She was full of admiration.

"Are you all right, Mrs. Dellrow?" Dr. Forbes asked.

Mary nodded.

"How about you, Lizabeth?"

"Yes." I'll never pretend to be a delicate swooning flower again, she thought. What in the world had I been thinking?

He patted the wound with alcohol and quickly wrapped a gauze bandage around it. Again, Lizabeth was impressed by his skill.

"Not too bad, Mrs. Dellrow. Keep it clean and let me see it in three days."

They watched Mary scurry out the door.

"It looks all right. A little longer and gangrene might have set in," Dr. Forbes said. "Do you think she'll come back?"

"I'll find some way to bring her." Lizabeth smiled. "Well, with a lot of help from my friends."

"You did beautifully, Lizabeth." He smiled. "As well as any medical technician."

His praise warmed Lizabeth. And suddenly a memory came rushing back. Poor Belinda, her favorite porcelain doll! She was forever breaking Belinda's arms and legs and setting them with splints of twigs and bandages. Mother would get upset at how destructive Lizabeth was. She didn't understand that Lizabeth was being a doctor. Poor forgotten Belinda was probably still wrapped in bandages somewhere in the attic. She'd had a head wound, too.

"I have another call to make," Dr. Forbes said. "The little Morrison boy with the croup, just a few doors from you. If you like, I'll give you a ride home."

"Thank you."

Lizabeth watched Dr. Forbes pack his black bag. What wouldn't she have given for a doctor's bag like that when she was seven! It was the last thing on earth her parents would have picked for a gift.

Rose, Amanda, and Kat were waiting in the outer room. They looked worried.

"Was it horrible?" Amanda asked.

"Do you feel all right?" Rose asked.

Lizabeth smiled. "In a way, it was . . . interesting."

"Lizabeth was a champ," Dr. Forbes said.

The other girls scattered and Lizabeth followed Dr. Forbes into his carriage. With a flick of the reins, the horse trotted along Lighthouse Lane.

"How is your family doing?" Dr. Forbes asked.

Lizabeth shrugged. She couldn't describe how lost they all were.

"Time heals," Dr. Forbes said. "People tell you that when they look for something to say, and maybe you can't believe it now but there's truth in it. Prayer helps, too."

Lizabeth nodded. Time and prayer, she thought, and doing something worthwhile.

"We've had no new cases this week," Dr. Forbes said. "Cape Light seems to be over the worst of it."

"Was it an epidemic, Dr. Forbes?"

"Bad as it was, I think we avoided a true epidemic. Cape Light folks were sensible and cooperative." He glanced sideways at Lizabeth. "Except for you—you took a big risk."

"I know," Lizabeth said, "but I'm not sorry."

The horse's hooves clopped on the pavement. They rode along in comfortable silence.

"It's a beautiful town," Dr. Forbes said. "I'm glad we came here."

"I'm glad you did, too," Lizabeth said. "I can't imagine Cape Light without Rose! And Dr. Forbes, Cape Light *needs* you."

"I'll try to live up to that," he said.

Dr. Forbes is easy to talk to, Lizabeth thought. So many grown-ups act stiff and distant with anyone young.

They were almost at the Merchant house when Lizabeth gathered her courage and asked, "Dr. Forbes, do you think I could be a doctor? Well, no, that's silly, isn't it? Women aren't doctors!"

"Did you ever hear of Elizabeth Blackwell?"

"No."

"She was the first woman to receive a medical degree. She graduated from Geneva College in 1849. Of course, that was after twenty-nine other medical schools rejected her."

"Then it's almost impossible."

"Not impossible. It's 1906 now, after all."

"What happened to her? Did she become a doctor?"

"Oh yes. Her younger sister Emily became a surgeon and they opened their own hospital in New York City. New York Infirmary for Women and Children, staffed entirely by women and serving the poor."

"What a wonderful thing to do!" Lizabeth said.

"You know, for a while I hoped Rose would follow in my footsteps." Dr. Forbes smiled. "But I think we've lost her to the horses."

"Do you honestly think I could?" Lizabeth asked. "I mean, a girl like me?"

"Perhaps not a *girl* but certainly a young *woman* like you. You'd have to have better grades than all the men. I know that's not fair, but maybe that will change by the time you apply, Lizabeth. Certainly if my wife has anything to say about it!"

So that's what being a suffragette was all about! "Then . . . then you don't think I should just forget about it?"

"Certainly not. Lizabeth, I'll encourage you any way I can."

"Could I—could I work for you, Dr. Forbes? I mean, as your assistant? Hold down arms and watch you?"

"No, I'm sorry." He had kind eyes. "You are a little young and not quite licensed yet."

"Oh. Of course. That was a dumb question."

"Not dumb," Dr. Forbes said. "Eager. If you're anxious to get started—my medical texts are too complex, but you could ask the Pelican Book Shop to get you a basic book on anatomy. You could see if you're really interested."

"I'll do that, Dr. Forbes!" If I do my best, I can get the grades, Lizabeth thought. Next term, I'll give *long* reports and win the spelling bee! My goodness, where was I all this time?

seventeen

izabeth was hurrying to meet Kat, Amanda, and Rose in the lighthouse tower. She was late. She had stopped off on the way.

She was almost there when she saw the light switching on. Its rays slowly revolved above the darkening town. It seemed to signal that all was well. The skirt of her new pink eyelet dress swirled around her legs as she rushed toward the welcoming beam. I'll always love pretty dresses, she thought, but there's a lot more on my mind now.

Kat, Amanda, and Rose were waiting in the tower room.

"What happened?" Kat asked. "We almost gave up on you."

"We saved some muffins for you," Rose said, "and that wasn't easy."

"Just proves we're true friends," Amanda said.

"They're so good. Blueberry."

"Sorry, I stopped off at the Pelican and I got into a conversation with Mrs. Cornell. She's so nice, I didn't want to cut her short. Anyway, a book I ordered finally came in. I've waited three weeks!" Lizabeth shifted the heavy volume to her other arm.

"Oh, good! Can I get it next?" Kat asked.

"I hope it's a romance," Amanda said. "I get seconds!"

Lizabeth laughed. "I don't think you'll want this one."

"Why? What is it?" Kat asked.

"*Basic Anatomy*," Lizabeth said.

"Say that again." Kat looked mystified.

"*Basic Anatomy*. I'm going to memorize all the bones."

"You're going to *what*?" Amanda asked.

"I was just remembering." Lizabeth went to the window and gazed at the waves hurling foam on the rocks below. "We've always shared our dreams up here. Since . . . since I don't know when."

"What does that have to do with *bones*?" Kat asked.

"My dream has changed," Lizabeth said. "Completely changed." She turned back to her friends and continued almost shyly. "I want to be a doctor."

"You mean *medical school*?" Rose asked.

Lizabeth nodded. "Well, after high school and college."

Her friends took a moment to let it sink in. Lizabeth was grateful that no one brought up the awful things she had said about women doctors—a few weeks and so very long ago. She hoped no one remembered.

"I'll have to get excellent grades to even hope to be admitted," Lizabeth said. "But I'm going to try my best. Starting next term."

"Hello? Is this Lizabeth Merchant speaking?" Kat asked.

"The *real* Lizabeth Merchant. Because . . . because that's what I truly want. Maybe what I've always wanted if I'd given myself a chance to think about it."

"You can do it if anyone can," Amanda said.

"Do you honestly think so?" Lizabeth asked.

"Of course you can!" Kat said. "You're extra-smart. Smarter than all of us put together." She grinned and added, "When you're not doing really dumb things."

Lizabeth smiled back. "I reserve the right to do something dumb once in a while."

"As long as you remember a doctor does *not* put night-shade in her eyes," Kat said. "It makes a bad impression."

The others looked puzzled.

"You should talk to my father," Rose suggested.

"I did. He's been giving me advice. Rose, he's wonderful!"

Rose smiled, pleased.

Kat looked thoughtful. "My dream hasn't changed. It's still art school, in Boston or New York, but I'm not just dreaming anymore. I mean, I'm saving up my gift paper money. I have time to do a *lot* of saving. And I'm finding out about scholarships."

"My dream is still horses," Rose admitted.

"Well, that's a big surprise." Amanda laughed.

"After high school, I'd love to have a ranch where I'd train and breed horses. Maybe out west. Mustangs and Palominos! And I'd have space to take in abused and abandoned carriage horses. What about you, Amanda?"

Amanda shrugged. "I guess I just want a husband and children someday."

They fell silent. Lizabeth was sure the others were thinking of Jed Langford, too, but no one mentioned him. Her father's disapproval made Amanda too unhappy.

"Now wait, Rose, before we leave your ranch in the west. Do you see a certain man among the horses?" Lizabeth teased.

Rose seemed to glow. "Chris likes the idea of ranching as much as I do. He loves the outdoors."

"You mean—have you actually talked about it?" Lizabeth was surprised.

"Well, yes. We talk about everything. A shared dream is the best kind."

"Does that mean you're serious? Are you engaged?" Lizabeth asked.

"We're too young to be *engaged*, but we're . . . I guess, engaged to be engaged to be engaged."

"I'm not even trying to figure that out," Kat said.

Rose smiled at Lizabeth. "Someday, I might be your sister. Only in-law, but—" She suddenly stopped and looked distressed.

"It's all right," Lizabeth said. "You're allowed to say the word 'sister' in front of me. You don't have to be so careful with me." Nothing anyone did would bring Tracy back, she thought. Maybe someday I'll learn how to heal other children. She shook off the sadness. "Forget 'in-law.' All three of you are my sisters in every way that counts."

"We were born a week apart," Kat said, "so Lizabeth and I are sort of twins."

Everyone broke into laughter.

"Surely not *identical.*" Lizabeth giggled.

"All right," Kat smiled, "maybe not."

"The four of us, sisters," Rose said. "I do like that."

"Four forever," Amanda said, "in our special place."

They stood hushed at the window. They held hands and looked out at the moon and the stars. The light slowly turned in its circle.

"Thank you, God," Lizabeth whispered. "Thank you for my friends and the happy times. Thank you for the strength to go on after the bad times. We'll face whatever life brings and we'll do it together."

"Together," Amanda, Rose, and Kat repeated.